ANTISENSE

&

Other stories

Jack Cohen

Copyright © Jack Cohen 2014

All rights reserved. No part of this book may be used or reproduced in any form whatsoever without the written permission of the author, except in the case of brief quotations or reviews.

This book is a work of fiction. All characters, scenes and dialogs are the products of the author's imagination. Any similarities to persons living or dead are entirely coincidental.

The cover design is by Jack Cohen and depicts DNA.

ISBN # 978-1499547238

Other works by Jack Cohen: "Amanuensis" (2009) "Discovering America" (2009); "Trove" (2009); "Confessions of a Jewish Activist" (2010)

www.jackcohenart.com
cohen.jack@yahoo.com

Elders of Zion Press

Contents

Antisense 1

Ulpan 83

The Perfect Spy 104

Jutland 131

Meningioma 140

Lesser Known Heroes of
Jewish History 152

    Leon Pinsker 155
    Pinhas Rutenberg 157
    Bronislaw Huberman 160
    Sholom Schwartzbard 163
    Morris "Two-Gun" Cohen 165
    Isaac Rosenberg 169
    Shmuel Zieglboim 171
    Leopold Trepper 172
    Solly Zuckerman 176
    Tuvia Bielski 180
    Richard Meinertzhagen 185
    Delmore Schwartz 187
    Josiah DuBois 189
    Zvika Greengold 193

Antisense

A story of discovery and intrigue in science

Contents

    Preface 2
1. Introduction 4
2. Antisense – Genetic Drugs ... 6
3. Antisense against AIDS 12
4. Moving to the NIH 18
5. Fateful decision 22
6. Sam Schwartz 24
7. Setting up the laboratory 28
8. The call from California 31
9. Lecturing 34
10. Akademgorodok 37
11. The Medicine Branch 43
12. Foxhall Road 47
13. Antisense Therapeutics Inc. .. 51
14. The falling out 55
15. Leila Subramanian 61
16. The grievance hearing 63
17. Sabotage 68
18. The CIA 70
19. Leaving NCI 74
20. Georgetown 77
21. Glossary 81

Preface

Science is revered in the western world as the rational subject par excellence. But, what people tend to forget is that science, the struggle for new knowledge and understanding, is in fact a human endeavor that suffers from all the same passions that both ennoble and degrade every other form of human activity. It is the content of science that is rational, not necessarily its human actors.

There are many well reported examples of how human attributes, such as jealousy, dislike and even hatred, as well as commercial rivalry, have influenced all forms of science. One example was the fact that Thomas Edison, who had invented direct current (DC) electricity, did everything he could to prevent his assistant Nikola Tesla from implementing and exploiting the preferable form of alternating current (AC) electricity, that subsequently became the norm throughout the world. Other examples were the barriers that were placed in the way of Albert Einstein and Sigmund Freud at several stages in their careers. It required confirmation over time for their then provocative theories to be accepted. That is the way of science.

Even less well-known scientists have experienced strong opposition, sometimes amounting to nasty innuendo, from older more established peers. One example was Dan Shechtman, who won the Nobel Prize for Physics in

2011, whose work on quasi-crystals was roundly rejected by such luminaries as Linus Pauling, whose own early work was considered just as revolutionary in its time.

In my own career, I experienced a great deal of personal animosity, petty jealousy and unpleasant behavior, on a far greater scale than my early training in Cambridge University prepared me for. Instead of the expected collegial atmosphere and cooperative attitudes, I encountered extreme rivalry, downright dislike, back-biting, name-calling and actual hatred. Surprised as I was to repeatedly discover this, I began to question my own character and the whole fabric of science. Certainly there are many who stop at nothing, including the manufacturing of results as well as the sensationalizing of mediocre results that provide false hope to many suffering patients. What was most upsetting was to find these attitudes present in abundance in the revered laboratories of one of the most famous scientific centers in the world, the National Institutes of Health (NIH) in Bethesda, Maryland.

1. Introduction

On a bluff overlooking the city of Bethesda, Maryland, just outside Washington DC, stands a huge conglomeration of buildings. This is the campus of the National Institutes of Health (NIH), the largest biomedical research centre in the world (**Figure 1**). It stands as a beacon of science protecting the health of the hinterland. Its campus is green and even beautiful in places, notwithstanding the huge glass and concrete structures. It is a temple to man's drive to conquer disease and live in good health.

The long corridors of its many buildings are busy with the tread of doctors, scientists, students and patients in a hive of focused activity. On the surface, all seems peaceful, yet in reality vicious turf wars for control of resources, for success and for power and fame are going on here. In this war there are winners and losers and incidentally sometimes cures for human diseases are also found.

There is a major dichotomy between the two main groups that work towards the elimination of disease, the scientists and the physicians. While the former seek the truth, searching for understanding and the mechanisms that underlie disease and the attempts to overcome it, the latter are more interested in "the cure." While the scientists deal with molecules and cells, the physicians have to deal with patients, some of whom are very ill or dying. Treatment at the Government run Clinical Centre that dominates the campus is free, but only to patients who are referred by their local physician because their disease is either rare or unusual or if they are terminal. So in the nature of things, the physicians rule the roost, they control the government hierarchy that runs the place, and they tend to treat the scientists as useful technicians.

This is a story of what goes on inside that impressive campus, behind the scenes, behind the facade. This is an account of scientific discovery, of human ambition, greed and betrayal.

Fig. 1. The campus of the National Institutes of Health (NIH) in Bethesda Maryland, USA, consisting of many disease-related research Institutes. The Clinical Center is in the foreground.

2. Antisense – Genetic Drugs

It was 1986. The door of my office was thrown open and in burst my two bosses, Ace Ericson, Head of the Clinical Pharmacology Branch, National Cancer Institute (NCI), and his boss Bernie Kaplan, Head of the Oncology Research Program, NCI. Bernie was at that time working very hard on trying to find an agent, any drug, that could counteract the effects of HIV, the causative virus of AIDS. He had worked on the first such anti-AIDS agent, namely AZT, work for which he had become famous. They were excited and had been arguing about a scientific paper they had seen in the literature. The paper that caught their attention was by someone I knew, Paul T'so (pronounced Cho) who worked at Johns Hopkins Medical School in Baltimore, Maryland.

Ace, known to all as Ace, had been very good to me. He had taken me into his department three years before, he had supported me, and had enabled me to set up my own research program, which was running quite successfully. He was a small man, with a bland face and a short sharp nose with piercing pale blue eyes. He had lank blondish hair that hung across the right side of his face. He usually wore a tie and jacket. He was a vegan and as far as I could tell he only ate dried vegetables, which explained his trim build and possibly his stoic personality.

Bernie Kaplan was quite different, he looked and sounded like Groucho Marx, except he was short without bending his knees. He had a Groucho moustache and round Groucho glasses. He was one of those important people who was too busy to stop working when you entered his office or if you encountered him in the hallway. He would say "talk to me" as he continued walking while reading a document. But, his intonation was so Groucho that I had to keep myself from laughing. But, he was a very serious and earnest clinician. He usually wore a pullover with a "v" neck. His favorite phrase was "lighten up."

The paper they were interested in described the use of short sequences of DNA known as oligonucleotides (shortened to oligos) to bring about the *selective regulation of gene expression*, an amazing feat if true (*oligo* means few, so an oligonucleotide contains a few of the basic units of DNA, or nucleotides, strung together). But, the oligos T'so used were not the natural units bound by phosphate bonds found in nature, since they would be easily degraded by enzymes called nucleases present in all cells to protect them against foreign DNA. He had used a chemically modified form called a *phosphonate*. Since I was the resident expert on phosphorus chemistry and DNA they came to me for clarification.

I had done my PhD on DNA and phosphorus chemistry in the laboratory of Lord Todd in Cambridge University, England. Lord Todd had won the Nobel Prize for his work on the synthesis of such important phosphate-containing compounds as ATP, the energy conserving component of cells, and had also proven the chemical structure of the nucleotide units of DNA that contain a phosphate group. I was therefore qualified to advise them. They wanted to know "what is antisense?" "what is a phosphonate?" and "why should it work?"

So I went to the blackboard and started to explain the whole process to them....

> *"Antisense* sounds technical but it really is simple. The base sequence that determines the function of DNA in the gene is called the *sense* sequence and the complementary sequence that binds to it through base pairing is termed the *antisense* sequence. By now most people know that DNA is the genetic substance and that it consists of a series of bases in a specific order. The bases are adenine (A), guanine (G), cytosine (C) or thymine (T). It was shown by Erwin Chargaff at Columbia University in the 1950s that the ratio of bases are such that A=T and G=C. Watson and Crick, when they determined the *double stranded helical structure* of DNA, used the results of X-ray diffraction of DNA fibers to determine that these so-called *base pairs* were the basis of the structure and around them spiraled the DNA backbone consisting of alternating sugar (deoxyribose) and phosphate groups. Since there are two strands the *sense* sequence was the name given to the strand that is used by the cell to synthesize proteins and *antisense* was the name given to the complementary sequence (**see Figure 2**).

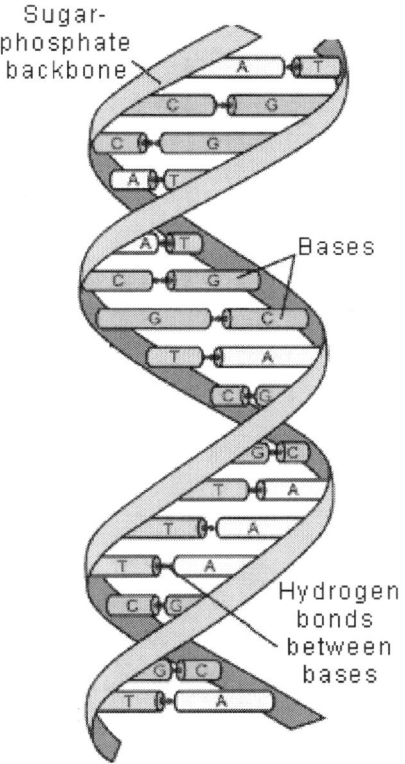

Fig. 2. Schematic diagram of DNA structure, showing the double helical structure with two strands, sense and antisense. The base pairs are in the center of the structure holding the two strands together and the backbone consists of an alternating sugar (deoxyribose) and phosphate chain. Hydrogen bonds hold the base pairs together. This model proposed by Watson and Crick in 1953, was subsequently confirmed by physicochemical studies.

Oligonucleotides or oligos are short sequences of the units of DNA chemically strung together. A breakthrough occurred when it became possible to synthesize them automatically using a machine called a *DNA synthesizer*.

Of course, the longer the sequence strung together the harder it is to synthesize it and the less the amount of product that is obtained. Short sequences of up to 15 units are optimal for research purposes."

It was a novel idea to use these short sequences of oligos as *antisense drugs*, the idea being that they would interact with their complementary sense sequence in the cell and thereby prevent a particular gene from being expressed into its gene product or protein. In a study published 14 years earlier, Paul Zamecnik and M.L. Stephenson had reported that they could kill the Rous sarcoma virus in cell culture using a specially selected sequence of bases, but their oligo had been made up of natural phosphate esters. Perhaps because of this, it was difficult if not impossible to repeat this work.

Using the *chemically modified forms of oligos* such as phosphonates (with a phosphorus-carbon bond) in place of phosphates (with phosphorus-oxygen bonds) would protect them from degradation by the prevalent nucleases in the cell (enzymes that degrade phosphorus-oxygen bonds but not phosphorus-carbon bonds) and allow the short sequences of DNA to be used as drugs. The attraction of this form of drug was that unlike the usual drugs which bind to proteins or enzymes and are all different, this form of drug binds to the messenger-RNA that takes the coding sense sequence into the cell and blocks its expression and so it could in principle be used against *any* genetic disease, including cancer. We called them "*genetic drugs.*"

After thus explaining this novel drug approach to my two bosses, I was given the immediate task, "see if you can synthesize such chemically modified oligos with the appropriate nucleotide sequence so that we can test them against the HIV virus."

You might ask, now why is this research against HIV being done in the National *Cancer* Institute? But, in fact HIV attacks the immune system thereby allowing many opportunistic infections, including some that lead to cancer. Also, in the face of the then growing epidemic of AIDS it was all hands on deck. Of course, there were other Institutes and groups doing AIDS research, including mainly the National Institute of Infectious Diseases, but many in the Cancer Institute were also focusing on that urgent problem.

But, the concept of antisense was in itself quite explosive. If you could *prevent the expression of a specific gene*, you had a new kind of drug, *a genetic drug* that could in principle *cure any genetic disease*. For such a golden concept people had struggled their whole lives and not succeeded. This was the stuff that dreams are made of, that people win Nobel Prizes for, and that could save innumerable lives.

3. Antisense against AIDS

Although Bernie had been successful in the development of AZT as an anti-AIDS drug (how successful is still a matter of controversy) he was still desperately searching for other more effective, agents. Together we agreed to test the *antisense method* against HIV.

This is what I did. I immediately took T'so's paper and rushed to the library to look up and get copies of the papers detailing the synthesis method. One of them was quite obscure, by a German author detailing the preparation of the necessary chemical precursors, and I had to search for this in the National Library of Medicine nearby. When I had got all the information together, I reviewed it and prepared a short report giving my proposed approach. In it I estimated how much the syntheses would cost for enough of the oligos, natural and chemically modified phosphonate versions, to carry out several tests against HIV with the necessary controls.

However, there was a catch, I did not have one of the new DNA synthesizers in my lab and there were none in the Oncology Program. I proposed to approach a friend in another lab on the NIH campus, Bob Henderson who had been a post-doc student of mine and who I knew had such a synthesizer in his lab, being tested in what is called "beta-testing," i.e. it was a prototype of a new commercial product. I would ask him to collaborate with us, but I proposed that we should immediately put in a request for such a machine ourselves so that we could be independent and so that we could obtain unlimited quantities of these oligos. I was immediately aware of the fact that we could also test them against other diseases with a genetic origin (note that the genetic origin of AIDS is the exogenous HIV virus, while the genetic origin of cancer is an endogenous oncogene). The catch of course was that these synthesizers were not cheap, each machine cost ca. $50,000.

I gave this brief proposal to Bernie, and he read it and immediately said, "go ahead!" I asked him about buying a DNA synthesizer, and he said "well, we're nearly at the end of the fiscal year, so prepare an order and get the official government pricing, and I'll see if we can push it through as part of the AIDS funding package."

There are two things to note here, first that often expensive equipment is ordered at the end of a funding cycle, when funds that are left over can be estimated and used most efficiently. The second crucial aspect, that was to affect my future career, was that I did not go through my immediate boss Ace Ericson, I went straight to his boss Bernie Kaplan. Now I did this because Bernie was the one working on AIDS and Ace was not. Also, I was an independent researcher and had been for many years, and since this was my area of expertise and not that of Ace, who was a clinical pharmacologist, I did not feel I needed his involvement. This was what could be called an elementary political mistake, one that carried the seeds of future disaster.

I went and visited my former post-doc Bob Henderson in his lab in another Institute at NIH and he was very cooperative, but he told me that the DNA Synthesizer was not really controlled by him, it was controlled by his friend and close collaborator Gordon Sunshine. They had a division of labor and he had taken the structural analysis of the products and Gordon had taken the synthesis.

But, it so happened that I knew Gordon Sunshine quite well, he had been Bob's collaborator when Bob had been working for me and Gordon had been an Assistant Professor at Catholic University of America in Washington DC. But, there Gordon had essentially no laboratory space, so I had allowed them to do a collaboration together using my lab space, particularly when I was away on sabbatical for a year. Gordon was very grateful for this and their successful work together had enabled them to get jobs working together at the NIH, with my recommendation. So Gordon was very receptive to my request for a collaboration, whereby he would synthesize the oligos we needed and I would supply them to Bernie for testing. This tended to make me a passive intermediary, but it was my knowledge and contacts that had initiated the project and I had every hope that within a reasonably short period of time I would have my own synthesizer running. Meanwhile I could learn a lot from Gordon (later he moved to California to work for the company making the DNA Synthesizers).

When you say that someone who runs a lab is going to collaborate with you, you know that he himself rarely actually does the bench work, Gordon had his post-doctoral fellow and I had mine and Bernie had his. So there are at least 6 people involved in this project that had yet to get off the ground. The cost for the precursors to synthesize the needed oligos would come from Bernie's major AIDS funding. In order to formalize the collaboration I wrote a memo that covered the work to be done by each group and distributed it to them.

In discussing the project with Gordon he told me that they were actively synthesizing some other chemically modified oligos that have a sulfur atom in place of an oxygen atom on the natural phosphate. They were doing this for structural analysis, but it immediately occurred to us that we could also test these analogues against HIV, and this was a serendipitous occurrence. Gordon agreed that his Japanese post-doc would synthesize the needed oligos, the natural phosphates (abbreviated PO) as controls, the phosphonates (abbreviated PM) as described by Ts'o and since they were working on them also the sulphur analogues, called phosphorothioates (abbreviated as PS).

I was naturally curious about their synthesis of the PS compounds that they had developed in collaboration with a Polish group. It turned out the synthesis was not working as well as expected, and the yields of the PS product were in fact only ca, 70%. This was not adequate for biological testing, so we agreed to see if we could improve the yield. The synthesis required heating of the reaction chamber of the synthesizer and this was proving difficult to do, leading to big variations in temperature and leaking from the joints. I knew a fellow who worked in the equipment design unit at NIH and so I went to him with this problem. He suggested some technical improvements and I paid for the making of the improved heated reaction vessel and with this (which took some weeks to get made) we were able to raise the yields of PS compound up to ca. 95%.

Meanwhile Gordon's Japanese post-doc Matsuo Shinokura had synthesized the natural PO oligo controls, then focused on the PM oligos, that proved quite difficult to make, and then when we had the improved heated reaction vessel, he made the PS oligos. It turned out that the PM oligos were very difficult to make since they were inherently insoluble in water. This was as a result of the substitution of the charged oxygen atom with a neutral carbon containing group, and the longer the oligos the less was the yield. By contrast, the PS compounds with a charged sulphur atom in place of a charged oxygen atom were still quite soluble. So we had three series of oligos to test.

I took these to Bernie's lab and gave them to his Japanese post-doc Kaito Matsura for the antiviral test against HIV. The theory was that if an agent killed the HIV virus selectively more than the controls then it might be an anti-AIDS drug, but if it had no effect then it was not worth taking further into more biological trials and into clinical trials on humans.

We were at this point unsure what would happen, it was after all a novel research project. As far as we were aware until then no such experiments had been done anywhere. Such is the nature of frontline pharmacological research against human viruses.

When we got the results we were flabbergasted, the PO oligo controls had no activity against HIV and this was not surprising, and the PM oligos also had no activity, but surprise, surprise, the PS oligos, that we had added as a second thought had high activity against HIV. We had inadvertently found a new potential anti-AIDS drug, and we were very happy. We quickly wrote a paper that was published in the *Proceedings of the National Academy of Sciences* (PNAS) in 1988 (note that it takes ca. a year for a paper to actually be published) and we made sure that the DNA Synthesizer order was expedited.

However, this work showed that the PS compounds had a non-sequence effect that was very worrying. In other words, in that HIV assay it didn't matter what PS oligo one used, they all had an inhibitory effect on the growth of HIV. It was still an anti-HIV agent, but we were looking for a sequence-specific antisense effect. So we changed the assay to another one that had been developed in Bernie's lab to search for a sequence-specific antisense effect.

4. Moving to the NIH

I had arrived at the NIH a few years before the antisense incident and had initially worked in the newly formed Division of Computer Research, even though I knew nothing about computers. This is how that happened.

I was invited to Washington DC by a colleague I had met once, who was aware of my work using the nuclear magnetic resonance (NMR) method to study proteins. At the time this was quite novel and he featured it in the symposium he organized for the American Chemical Society. While I was in DC I went and visited the NIH to meet other colleagues who I knew there.

One of them told me that the Computer Division, which at that time had lots of money to buy computers, had agreed to buy the latest NMR machine, that cost ca. $250,000, which no other institute could afford, And there was a position going with the machine to run it and bring data into the computer division that the director of the division wanted to have.

So I applied for the job, was interviewed and got the job. This involved moving to Bethesda MD outside Washington DC. At first we rented a nice townhouse in Rockville MD and I drove about 15 mins to work. The new NMR machine was located in an old building in the basement and I had a lab there, but my office was in the Computer Division. Paddy Scott, the colorful Head of the Computer Division didn't want to just give the money for the machine, he wanted data from it to be brought into the Division and analyzed there using the computer capabilities.

I generated data on proteins, put it on computer cards and read it into the large IBM computer and then found myself sitting at a console where I could retrieve the data and see it on the monitor. This was one of the first such interactive set-ups. Then I analyzed the data theoretically and this led to the publication of several papers.

I was happy with this arrangement, although it was not entirely convenient. One day I learnt that the Computer Division that had been set up by a separate act of Congress, was going to be incorporated into the rest of the NIH and research would not be allowed there. I went to see Paddy Scott about his, and at first he would not see me. So I told his secretary that I would sit outside his door until he did. Finally he saw me and confirmed that as a result of the changes my position would no longer be available. Since I was just in the process of buying a house I was desperate, I pleaded with him to help me find a position elsewhere at NIH.

He agreed to do this, and while I was sitting in his office he called the heads of other institutes and asked them if they had a position for a talented researcher, specializing in biological NMR studies.

Quite independently a friend of mine had decided to learn how to sword-fight. He went to evening classes and there met a friend who worked in the NCI. He told this man about me and that I was looking for a job in NIH and this man then told the head of his division about me, and the next day coincidentally he received a call from Paddy Scott about me. So he asked me to come over for an interview, and that's how lives are changed.

I had set up my lab in the Clinical Pharmacology Branch on the sixth floor of the main Clinical Center at NIH two years before to do mainly physicochemical studies of the differences between drug resistant and drug sensitive cancer cells. But, now that I had this new antisense project, I needed more space and more people. Since we now had a date for the delivery of the DNA synthesizer I needed another lab, since the one I had was already full and busy.

Fortunately Bernie was in charge of the space and forced Ace to give me another lab across the corridor where I could accommodate the DNA Synthesizer (which took up half a bench) as well as the chemicals needed to run it. I also needed a technician to run it, and a post-doc to work with me on the project.

I was given these two slots to fill, something that was like discovering gold in a long-neglected mine. I went about looking for appropriate candidates for this project. I soon found a young woman to be the technician, she was of Indian origin and her name was Leila Subramanian. She was very enthusiastic and energetic and I liked her from the start. She proved to be a very good choice.

5. Fateful decision

I stood poised before the white Formica desk, my back to it, facing Ace Ericson, my boss, head of the Clinical Pharmacology Branch. He said "I know you have a place in your lab, and I have a great candidate for you." I remained in a defensive posture, unsure how to respond to his suggestion.

Over time our relationship had subtly changed and I realised that he was somewhat upset with me, which I thought was due to the fact that I had not included him in my research and in my publications. I could understand why he might be resentful at not being included in the antisense research that had great potential for future drug discovery. I instinctively thought that this new candidate might be a "Trojan horse" inserted into my lab to find out what I was doing. These thoughts ran through my head as I tried to answer him in a neutral manner. "Who is the candidate?" I inquired, "and what is his background?"

"His name is Sam Schwartz and he has a PhD in chemistry as well as being an oncologist, and when he approached me for a job, I immediately thought of you. He did his PhD with a well known man out in California, and I told him about your antisense work and he is very interested in that. He is a clinical fellow and it won't cost you anything to have him in your lab, as the Department will support him. He is waiting outside and he is eager to meet you. Since your lab is the most appropriate for him in the Department I would very much like you to take him in."

My mind was racing, considering the options, because even at this stage, I did not fully trust Ace. Nor did I have any idea who this new candidate was, this Trojan horse. In order to play for time I asked, "can I see his cv, and could he give a seminar so that I can see how he presents and the level of his work?" Ace answered, "sure, I'll get him to give you his CV, and we'll arrange for him to give a lab seminar on his chemical work. Now, shall I call him in so you can meet him?" Of course I said "yes", I felt as if I owed Ace a lot, and I could not say "no" directly to him, but I had a bad feeling.

I shook hands with the candidate, Sam Schwartz, and we exchanged pleasantries. He was from New York, he apologized that his chemistry was a bit rusty since he had been a medical student for many years, but he would brush up on his Thesis work and he would be happy to give a seminar on it. Soon he gave me his CV, which was not so impressive, but he gave a reasonable seminar, and I could see no overt reason to reject him. So in 1988, Sam Schwartz entered my lab as a clinical fellow to do a research project in the area of antisense oligonucleotides as anti-cancer drugs. This was a decision I would later live to regret.

6. Sam Schwartz

Sam Schwartz was a short, stocky figure, almost as wide as he was tall. His head seemed somewhat too large for his body, and presented a macrocephalic aspect, with his jaw and forehead jutting forward, the kind of thing one sees in athletes who have taken too much steroid. This can also be a natural condition produced by having too much growth hormone during development. His prognathus jaw gave him a slightly menacing appearance, and his tendency to having red blotches over his face made him seem unnatural. His fingers were stubby and he tended to twirl them in front of his chest when he was sitting and talking.

As soon as he arrived in the lab, he placed a stereo tape recorder on the shelf in front of his desk, with a stack of music tapes next to it. Although these tapes were of classical music I never actually heard him playing them, like much else in his personality they were for show. He also placed a brass Indian wheel representing the wheel of life with the figure of an Indian deity on it. I soon realized from his demeanor that these were symbols of his need to impress.

The layout of the office was that there were benches covered in white Formica on each side. However, on the left there was a small safety door between the office and the adjoining lab, so that someone could escape in case of fire. This meant that there were spaces for three people to sit at desks on the right-hand side, but only two on the left. Sam occupied the place at the end on the right next to the door, between him and my small office at the end sat my Indian post-doc Satcharya Ram. On the other side, were the Dutch guy Otto van Rijn, the Japanese fellow Nomi Edoh and the British chap Walter Hazen, altogether a very international bunch. Life is too short to describe the mutual interactions and often humorous encounters between this group of post-docs. Note that Hazen was a pediatrician, and they are usually the nicest of docs, and he never got along with Sam Schwartz.

At least in my tiny office I had a window overlooking part of the campus, since we were on the 6th floor, and I had a door that I could slide shut if I wanted to have privacy. But generally I kept the door open, so that there would be a sense of openness in our relationships and I tried to foster good communications between the fellows so that they could both feel at home and could learn from each other. Each one of them had a separate project, some of them on similar topics, and it was my practice when each joined the lab to not only go over the project I was proposing for each of them, but also to follow up with a detailed memo outlining the project and the experimental approach that would be needed to accomplish it. Naturally, I also did this for Sam Schwartz when he joined the lab. I also told him and Leila that she should help Sam by synthesizing oligos for him at first, but that he should learn how to do this for himself as part of his research.

I became Sam's confidante, he would come to me and tell me stories without any prompting from me and without any reciprocation. On one occasion, Sam came to my sliding door and pulled it close next to him and opened his lab coat and showed me a wad of $100 bills. I asked "where did you get those from?" and he said "one of the patients from New York was very grateful that I got their daughter into the NCI protocol." Although I was not a clinical oncologist like him, I knew that it was strictly illegal for him to take money from a patient at NIH. But, at the time I did nothing about it.

Sam used to regale me with stories of his doings, some that were downright weird. For example, a well-known couple in the Jewish community of Virginia got into financial difficulties, leading to tension, leading to murder. The wife shot the husband dead, claiming that he was stealing their money and having affairs with prostitutes. She was arrested. This was all reported in the newspaper. They lived in a large house in the affluent suburb of McLean. Realizing that there would be no one at home, since the husband was dead and the wife incarcerated, Sam rented a large truck, and with a nefarious friend, drove to their house, broke in and during one dark night removed all their furniture and belongings into the truck. He used the furniture to furnish the basement in his house and the rest he sold and made a lot of money off it. He said, "Well, they certainly don't need it anymore!"

Sam had one very annoying habit, he liked to snoop around, find out what was going on and then call me, very often in the evening around 6 -7 pm just as I was eating dinner, to tell me the latest scuttlebutt and rumors going around. What Ace had said to whom, whose status was high and whose low, whose work was going well and who had problems. Out of about 30 post-docs I had never had one who had ever done such a thing before. I tolerated these calls, but my wife was very annoyed by them and said "you mark my words, this person is trouble!"

7. Setting up the laboratory

Our collaboration with Gordon Sunshine was going well and they were churning out oligos for HIV testing, but then Gordon came to me because he had a problem. His post-doc position was for only one year and it was due to run out in a few months, and if he could not find other support his Japanese post-doc Matsuo Shinokura would have to return to Japan. Gordon's boss had told him that there were no funds to renew it, and without him Gordon would not himself be able to run the synthesizer and provide the oligos for the research. I immediately went to Bernie and told him the situation and pointed out that we would soon have delivery of our own DNA synthesizer, whereupon we would no longer be dependent on Gordon Sunshine, but, we would need our own post-doc to continue the research.

This was providential, if he could get me the post-doc position, then Matsuo could simply transfer to my lab and continue the work. He agreed, so this was very fortuitous for me. In addition I had the technician Leila Subramanian who would do the routine work of making sure the machine was supplied with the necessary chemicals and was kept running efficiently to output as much oligos as possible. Both of these two, Leila and Matsuo, would sit in the laboratory with the DNA synthesizer.

Sure enough during this time using a different HIV assay we then discovered a *sequence-specific antisense effect*, but only for the PS oligos, so we wrote another paper for FNAS and when this was published in 1989 we were *very* happy. Also, in 1989 I edited and published the first book on the subject of *"antisense oligos as selective inhibitors of gene expression."*

At the time it really did not occur to me that Ace, who was technically my boss, would resent my success with this antisense work and also my direct relationship with his boss, Bernie. After all, we were scientists and the ideal was to pursue knowledge, defeat disease, publish papers and if possible achieve fame. But, I must admit that I deliberately excluded him form this work, because after all he made no contribution to it. So we also went ahead and applied thru the office of Patents at NIH for a patent for our work on antisense agents against HIV

At that time NIH, being a government institution, did not have its own patent attorneys, but farmed out the work to private attorneys under contract. I had a visit from a patent attorney who was very old, smelt of alcohol and seemed incompetent. He wrote a draft that I found totally inadequate and so I complained and he was replaced and this all took time.

Meanwhile I knew that others had seen our papers in PNAS and were busy competing on the same subject. However, for a patent what matters is when the work was done, and many years later when the patent was subsequently granted to NIH, it was disputed by another group. We were able to show to the patent judge's satisfaction that we did not copy our competitor's work, but rather they copied ours. Nevertheless, although this was important and involved a lot of money for NIH, we got only a very small percentage of the payments to NIH from private companies that were set up to try to develop antisense drugs commercially.

8. The call from California

One morning when I was in the lab I received a call from California, from someone who said he had seen our abstract in the current scientific meeting that was going on in San Diego, where Bernie's Japanese post-doc was presenting our work. When the caller had approached this fellow he had referred him to me as the antisense expert and he said anyway his English was poor and he couldn't understand him properly. He asked me if he could come out and speak to me, and I said yes, of course, and he said, "I'll be there tomorrow."

This blew me away, no one had ever taken any particular interest in my work and none had ever come out from California on a day's notice to speak to me. I had always wanted to be involved in some great adventure, some great task, and suddenly here it was. I had found my niche, I had struck gold.

Charles Brundy when he came was a revelation. He was the golden boy from the West Coast, he was salvation itself. He told me that he worked for a venture capital company in Palo Alto, that he had degrees in biology and business and was a qualified MD. But, he had not practiced medicine, instead he was looking for a novel drug development program to invest in, and he was sure he had found it in antisense. He asked me many questions about antisense and then invited me to help form a company with him.

Of course, it would mean leaving NCI, but it was very uncertain, there was enough money to get thru the first year, but after that we would need an injection of venture capital funds. My role would be scientific director and I would have founder's shares in the company, but it was clear that he would control the finances and I could not expect much salary until the company achieved some success. I thought about it, then demurred. I told him that I was a researcher, I was primarily an academic and that I could not see myself in such a role. It would mean giving up a stable job for unknown prospects.

He said, "don't decide immediately, I'll be in touch with you and you can then give me your answer, meanwhile I want you to be a consultant to the company." A few days later he called me, as I was having a dinner out with friends at a Chinese restaurant, and on the phone I turned down his offer. Nevertheless, he invited me out to California a few times, and paid me handsomely for advice, about whom I thought would make a good DNA chemist, who would be a good DNA synthesizer technician, etc.

He did in fact employ as chief chemist one of the people I recommended, although this person was a rival of mine and indeed was very negative about everyone else's work. The last time I went out to see him, after a nice meal in a fancy restaurant up in the redwood hills, he drove me back to the airport in his MG sports car and told me that he intended to build a billion dollar company, and in fact he did. I've always wondered what would have happened if I had accepted his offer.

9. Lecturing

Up to the time I started working on antisense, which involved my knowledge of nucleic acids based on my PhD Thesis at Cambridge University, I had worked mainly on protein structure using NMR, nuclear magnetic resonance spectroscopy. Without going into the technical details NMR had revolutionized the determination of the structures of chemical substances, and I was intrigued by the prospect of applying it to the structure determination of proteins.

I worked in this area for several years and published many papers, and it seemed very successful, yet I knew that it was not a very fashionable subject. Structure determination of proteins had been carried our very successfully by X-ray crystallographers who had determined the actual structures of many proteins that could be crystallized, and Max Perutz had even won the Nobel Prize for the determination of the structure of hemoglobin, the oxygen carrying protein in the blood. Now NMR provided a way to determine the structure in solution, but there were limits on the size of the protein that could be determined and one needed large amounts of stable proteins, significant limitations. I was very glad to have the opportunity to return to DNA research.

My antisense research attracted quite a lot of attention and I began to be invited more regularly, about once a month, to give seminars and lectures at various conferences and universities. One day I received an invitation to lecture at the University of Pennsylvania at the Johnson Foundation. This was the Department of my esteemed colleague Mildred Cohn, and of the head of the Foundation, Britton Chance. Britton Chance was a very well-known researcher and formidable intellect, whose work had unfortunately come into question. He studied brain metabolism and had been using the state-of-the-art method called "freeze-clamp," whereby a mouse or rat brain was treated in a certain way and then suddenly frozen to liquid nitrogen temperature in a metal clamp. The brain was then dissected and studied.

However, the results obtained for the level of ATP for example, which is the major source of energy in the cells, was much less than obtained by another method, phosphorus NMR, which did not require the destruction of the brain itself. It was realized that the sudden freezing of the brain caused the formation of ice particles, that breached the cell walls and released an enzyme that degraded ATP, thus giving lower results. When this was revealed by experiment, Britton Chance, instead of defending his former results, showed great resilience and changed his research to using phosphorus NMR,

Anyway, I had spent the weekend with friends in New Jersey and decided to drive back via Philadelphia to give the lecture. I started out early enough and consulted a map. I saw that there was a large road that ran almost parallel with the Philadelphia beltway rte I295 and since I thought I had enough time I decided to take this route into the city. I soon realized that this was a big mistake, since the road was not continuous and took me thru not only suburbs, but also thru the black ghetto area. At one point I got lost, and had to stop to ask the way. The black guys who directed me looked at me strangely, who was this crazy white ass with the strange accent who dared to trespass into their domain. Little did they realize that I had grown up in a worse slum than theirs.

I realized that this was taking a lot longer than I had expected and barely got to the University on time. I found a parking spot and raced into the building barely 5 min before the lecture was due to start. Then I put my slides in the tray just in time.

Early on in my career, like most people, I had an aversion to public speaking. This was especially difficult when you had only 10 or 15 min to tell a story and you had to measure every word. Later I developed a stratagem to ensure that I don't arrive late for a lecture, out of 100 points, I give myself 50 for getting to the right place and another 25 for being there on time, then 15 are for having the slides ready in a carousel for showing, and the remaining 10 are for actually giving the lecture. This makes sure that I take getting there on time seriously and means that I don't feel so much pressure for actually giving the lecture. On several occasions I was invited to give plenary lectures at meetings of the Am. Assoc. for Cancer Research, to halls of maybe a thousand people, and this strategy helped me considerably to overcome any jitters.

10. Akademgorodok

Knowledge about the antisense work started to spread and I was invited to speak at many conferences and give seminars in many universities. It was good to have one's research recognized, and of course, I gave credit to my collaborators and my post-docs.

As antisense came to be known in the scientific community companies were established to exploit the potential. There were companies in Boston, New York, San Francisco, Toronto, and even in Paris. These companies involved the investment of millions of dollars in expensive research. I was invited to lecture and/or consult at some of these, and it certainly increased my income. However, I had to inform the NIH of all my earnings from lectures and it had to be done on my own time.

There were specific conferences organized on the subject. The first one was a small affair in Annapolis, Maryland. I organized the second one near NIH in June 1989, and it was a crowded and very exciting affair. Then there were follow-up meetings in Paris (very elegant), in Les Arcs in the French Alps (couldn't learn to ski), in Colorado, and in other choice spots on the earth.

The one that most piqued my attention was the invitation I received to go to Akademgorodok, near Novosibirsk in Siberia, for a small conference on antisense. This was quite surprising since Akademgorodok or "science city" had been a closed area and this was apparently only the second conference that they were going to have open to visitors from outside the Soviet Union. Naturally, I applied as required thru the usual channels to go to this conference. Unfortunately I was told that there were no funds available for this trip, and I did not have any funds of my own to pay for it.

I was very disappointed at this, since it would have been a great experience to visit the USSR during this early period of opening up of "perestroika" under Pres. Gorbachev in 1988. I mentioned this invitation to others in the lab, and then heard to my surprise that Sam Schwartz had also applied to attend this conference and had been given permission to go, which he proudly boasted to all within earshot. It was unheard of for an inexperienced post-doc to be chosen to go to a conference ahead of his supervisor who had been specifically invited.

So naturally I went and complained to Ace. But, he told me that the Institute was not paying for Sam, he was paying out of his own funds. I then told Ace about the money that Sam had shown me that he had received from a patient that I knew was bankrolling his trip. Ace was not shocked and appeared to know about it. I told him if Sam goes and I don't, I will go to Brian Cranmer, the Head of the Institute, and tell him about this.

Ace said he would see what he could do. In the end, Sam was forced to return the money (I was told) and we were both given permission to go to the Russian meeting at NCI's expense.

It was quite exciting to fly to Moscow, where we stayed in the drab guest house of the Academy of Sciences, and then fly on to Novosibirsk, a long and tedious flight over vast and undeveloped forests. The food on board was atrocious and the pilot must have been a fighter plane veteran. From Novosibirsk we were taken by coach a few hours ride along rutted roads to the science city, Akademgorodok.

This was a city in a forest of ash trees with large grand buildings of institutes of all kinds of sciences along wide boulevards and utilitarian housing blocks. We stayed in the only hotel in the city, which was quite basic.

The meeting that was held at the Institute of Physicochemical Biology was small and quite intimate and we knew most of the foreigners there, but few of the Russians. Our host, Yuri Osipov, who was working on antisense, proved to be charming and helpful, and at a party at his house, after drinking numerous toasts, he told us stories against the Soviet system that I never expected to hear inside the USSR. In fact, he was so negative that I considered the possibility that he was an *agent provocateur*.

He told us that his father had eaten too much one day and got a blockage of his intestine. Yuri had taken him to the local hospital and told the doctor on duty the problem. The doctor had indignantly replied, "we do the diagnosis here, not the patients," and had thrown him out of the emergency room. When he came back the following morning he was told his father was dead! It appeared that nothing was done to remove the blockage and his father had died during the night. In a normal country there would have been a case of negligence, but not in the USSR.

It seemed that the head of the hospital was a friend of the wife of a high party official and so his position came from influence not from ability. Further, this Party official's wife was a believer in the healing properties of the sun, so every day patients in this hospital were dragged out of bed to sit in the sunshine, even when it was freezing cold outside. There was nothing anyone could do about it.

One day we went to visit Novosibirsk. Since I had contacts with Jewish groups in the West who were working for the release of Soviet Jews, I asked if there were any refuseniks there, people who had applied to leave but were refused, and lost their jobs and income. I was asked by my contacts to visit two people in Novosibirsk who were on their lists, whom no one had ever visited before. I decided to go on the day we had off from the conference, and Sam asked to join me.

We eventually found the small apartment of one of the people. He was very intense, for he had found religion, the Jewish religion I mean, and had been ostracized by all around him. He and his wife were waiting and praying for the time when they would be allowed to leave the Soviet Union for Israel. He had grown a long beard and it was surprising to find the picture of the Lubavich Rebbe on the wall in that god-forsaken place. He pressed me for money and I gave him some, but Sam, of course, did not.

Later we found the apartment of the other person, but he was out and his wife was very cagey, she suspected a trick, when two foreigners came knocking on her door in remote Novosibirsk. So she wouldn't let us in, but I wrote a note for her husband in English that she promised to give to him.

While we were making our way back to the train station, Sam had a terrible stomach ache, and there was no toilet in sight. We walked around asking for one in bad Russian and people looked at us as if we were crazy. Finally we spotted a building that turned out to be the local college, and we asked to enter. At first the guard at the gate would not let us in, but when we showed him our passports and Sam started to bellow in pain, he finally relented and so let us in. We found the toilets from the stench, they were open and filthy and I stayed away from them, but Sam had no choice.

While he was busy there I wandered along the corridor and found a small group of students sitting on the floor in a tiny bare room, where they were talking and smoking and one was playing a guitar. I was struck by how primitive and basic it all was, no lights, no paint on the concrete walls, no bookcases, no books, no desks, nothing. I tried to chat with them for a while until Sam returned from purgatory, cursing the dreadful state of the facilities.

I had brought a Groucho Marx false nose, glasses and moustache, with me that I wore to the social event at the Conference, and it was received with stony looks by the Soviets. I said it was my Karl Marx disguise, but they didn't find it funny. Then I realized that they had no idea who Groucho Marx was, they had never heard of the Marx Brothers. What a bust!

At the conference I had noticed a particularly beautiful young woman, with a blond braid and blue eyes, who was one of the Russian students at the conference. She, like all of them, was eager to test her English on us and we were soon chatting away. She sat near us at the final conference dinner, where toasts were exchanged and I had to give one. I learned later that Sam had offered her a position in his lab (that strictly speaking he did not have) in the States and that later she did in fact join him.

11. The Medicine Branch

Mort Feldman was the Head of the Medicine Branch, the largest Branch in the NCI. He was an internationally known expert in Breast Cancer and was highly respected and even feared because he had such a demanding personality. It was known to be inadvisable to get on his wrong side, but in my few interactions with him he had always been pleasant to me.

Apparently he was dissatisfied with the state of the NCI and its leadership, so after some internal dissension he decided to leave. It was front page news in *The Washington Post* when he left NCI and took 30 of his researchers with him to the Lombardi Cancer Center at Georgetown University Medical School, in nearby Georgetown in Washington DC. This was an unprecedented event.

This left the Medicine Branch without a Head, and so a nation-wide search was instituted to find his replacement. However, it proved very difficult because salaries in the federal government were a fraction, perhaps a third or less, of the salaries available in the private medical world. Further, this was a very responsible job with a huge load of work with perhaps 50 clinical fellows under him, as well as research responsibilities. Two candidates were found, but eventually their applications fell through.

As a result they started looking within NCI for a replacement for Feldman, but no-one obvious presented was available. Eventually in desperation, as a fifth choice, they asked Ace Ericson if he would take the job. This was a big surprise, because Ace was not a practicing oncologist, but rather a pharmacologist, and it smacked of desperation, because anyone who knew Ace knew that he was ambitious but not very efficient.

I was friendly with Ace's secretary, a nice old Jewish lady, named Gertrude, who was always nagging him to get to his meetings on time, and running after him to sign urgent letters. I spoke to her about his becoming the Head of the Medicine Branch and she said it would be a disaster.

One day when I was in the office, Ace came in and sat down and said he wanted to talk to me. He then embarked on a listing of all the advantages of his becoming the Head of the Medicine Branch, and then he asked me to tell him truthfully what I thought. I told him that I thought it would be a big mistake for him. I couldn't say that he was barely managing to run the Pharmacology Branch and that was a lot smaller. Also, he had no experience organizing a clinical program with so many people. But, I intimated that it would be too much responsibility and take too much time for him.

Then he disclosed a bombshell, if he took the job he intended to combine the Medicine and the Pharmacology Branches. I thought this was a completely crazy idea, to combine two such distinct Departments, one research-oriented and the other clinical. Anyway, although I was negative about this, he didn't seem to be interested in my opinion, it seemed that he had already made up his mind and was merely telling me in advance. I realized immediately that this could not bode well for the Pharmacology Branch and for my lab in particular.

When Ace took the job the Branch office now moved from the 6th floor to the 8th floor and we saw much less of him. But, sometimes I had to go up there, and one day I was present when a strange scene unfolded. A young woman, a Clinical Fellow, came into the office and asked to see Ace. The Secretary called him on the intercom and then told her he was unavailable. She became very agitated and insisted, and then went to his office door and pulled it open and started to have a loud argument with him. He came out into the main office and they went at it. She told him that he had no right to switch schedules and that she had to go to her brother's wedding and he had changed her time slot without consulting her and she simply could not accept that. While they were thus going at it, he insisting that she had no choice, another Fellow came into the office and got involved in the argument and agreed that the organizing of the clinical schedule was arbitrary and insensitive. He said that he was also not consulted when changes were made in the schedule. The woman became very emotional and said "I'm going to my brother's wedding and as far as I'm concerned you can fire me," and she stormed out. This only took a few minutes, but I had never seen such a scene as that before at NIH.

I knew it was symptomatic of the lack of efficient organization that Ace was known for, especially as he now had two Departments under his direction. No wonder he wanted to integrate them. I heard thru the grapevine that Ace was hurting for senior positions in the Medicine Branch and I realized that by combining the two Branches he would be able to transfer my position into the Medicine Branch. I knew that my days were numbered, especially since my research did not also involve Ace.

12. Foxhall Road

Through the most salubrious part of the suburban area of Washington DC called Potomac, runs the narrow winding road called Foxhall Road. Along its length are the mansions of the very rich, those who live in a different realm than the rest of us. For example, one of the estates is owned by the Kreeger family and they have a private art gallery at 2401 Foxhall Road that is open to the public at certain times. It contains several impressionists and other valuable artworks.

One of the residents of Foxhall Road was a lady named Georgina Lavelle, a well-connected, wealthy, influential lady, who gave large donations to cancer research and bank-rolled the American Cancer Organization. It was said that a Director of NCI could not be selected without her agreement. She became interested in antisense and I was introduced to her by Brian Cranmer, the Director of the NCI. She exuded charm and affluence. When I met her in his offices she was wearing a grey suit with an over the shoulder jacket with a thin fur scarf attached, with a large shiny black handbag and a small black fitted hat. She was an older woman, but she was striking!

It was clear that everyone deferred to her, and she had a companion who was apparently her business manager or something like that. We sat down and then she asked me to explain antisense to her. I did my bit, and then she cross-questioned me. She was really sharp and knew her stuff. Her business partner also weighed in. I gave them the names of companies that were pursuing antisense and those that were being formed, and I told them about the people involved in these ventures, including my estimates of their capabilities and their potential. Of course, there were several approaches one could take, not only the *PS-oligos* that I had worked on. Other researchers were pursuing synthetic *ribo-oligos* and so-called *ribozymes* that were DNA oligomers that had been selected for catalytic activity against target mRNA, *and triplex formation*, the formation of triple helical segments of DNA that could reduce gene expression. There were also attempts to improve cellular uptake of oligos as well as making oligos with attached chemically active groups to "knock-out" the complementary mRNA. All this was fascinating and indicated a new field of drug development that was in ferment that was attracting millions of dollars of investment money. They seemed to be suitably impressed.

Although this meeting left me with a kind of high, I reflected that my expertise was being used for their personal gain, without me getting anything out of it. Also, it seemed inappropriate that this meeting should occur in a government office where private investment matters were obviously being considered. I decided to raise these considerations with Bernie Feldman, who had arranged this meeting.

The following week I received a call asking me to stop by at the home of Mrs. Lavelle on Foxhall Road. I arranged a convenient time when I was off work and went to her home. It was a huge mansion with its own driveway. A maid let me in and asked me to wait in the reception room. It contained a library and pile of handsome coffee table books. Next to them on the glass table was an open bible in a stand that I looked at and realized was an authentic ancient version.

The business manager came in and introduced himself again. He expressed his and Mrs. Lavelle's thanks for my splendid interview with them the previous week. He then gave me an envelope that contained a check and asked me to sign a nondisclosure form that meant that our conversations would be privileged and they would like me to continue advising them in this difficult and technical area. For any further communications they would continue to express their gratitude accordingly. Of course, I was glad to accept.

When I had signed the form, he took it and left and then Mrs. Lavelle came in and the maid served tea and we had a nice chat about her books and her interests in supporting cancer research and her travels and so on. It was all very convivial, but I had a bad feeling at the back of my head. I realized that I was being used to help advise their investments in front line research in cancer, but on the other hand I was being paid for it and who could complain. She was certainly very pleasant and took the time to "get to know me."

Sometime later I was invited to a dinner at her home. It was rumored that at these dinners she chose people who would later be promoted as leaders of the NCI and other cancer organizations. It was a very lavish affair, held in a large dining room with many servants, most of them black, done in the old fashioned way. Wives were also invited and we had a very nice time, chatting and drinking and eating to our heart's content.

13. Antisense Therapeutics Inc.

I was expecting some follow-up to this meeting and indeed I was soon approached by a venture capital firm in New Jersey, who told me that they wanted to start a company focusing on antisense. I was invited to go up to New York and deliver a lecture at a private meeting in a hotel. I was well prepared, but I must say this was somewhat intimidating, different to any other lecture I had given. I was interrupted and questioned by a small audience of eminent experts in various fields related to cancer. One of them was a leading world famous researcher from a New York institution, and others were well known to me.

After my presentation, the host, an imposing man named Wallace Levine who had been the director of research at one of the leading pharmaceutical companies, cross-examined me. He asked such questions as what would I do if such and such a thing happened? What is your plan B? Suppose the antisense approach doesn't pan out, suppose it's due to poor cellular uptake or an adverse human reaction, or …and so on. Of course, I had few answers to these conjectural questions. Nevertheless at the end of the exhausting day, the committee voted to approve the formation of a company to carry out drug development studies in the antisense area.

The next step was to find someone who could be the CEO of the company, since I had no such experience I was not a candidate for this position, but I was asked to be Scientific Director. Since this would require me to leave NCI and become an actual company employee I turned it down, but instead I was asked to be the scientific advisor of the company, so that I could still remain at NCI, and I received a handsome financial agreement with the venture capital company. Of course, I knew that other such companies had been founded or were in the process of being formed. I discussed this with Wally and he pointed out that there is a "window of opportunity" for such a venture. We were still in that window, but it would soon close, and then there would be a winnowing out process, whereby those companies that had pursued a dead end, or were not well run, or did not get further funding, would fail. We must make sure that didn't happen to our company. It was named Antisense Therapeutics Inc. and was located in New Jersey.

According to the agreement I signed with them I had to help with writing the business plan for the company, help with recruiting suitable employees, outline the research plan and attend monthly meetings in New Jersey to monitor the progress of the research program. It was quite a challenging experience to do all this and continue my other research. I also had to request permission from NCI to carry out these activities and receive the consultation fees. This was granted under the new regulations that allowed researchers to help the formation of biotech start-up companies that were seen as the new way forward. In effect, the government funded research was seeding the development of a whole industry of new start-ups.

Wally called me and said he thought they had found a perfect candidate to be CEO of Antisense Therapeutics; Bradford Singer was the head of a department at one of the leading pharmaceutical companies located in NJ and he wanted to leave to start his own biotech company. I was asked to go up to NY to be present at his formal interview. He was great as far as I was concerned, well-informed, experienced and smooth. I voted yes and he was offered the job.

Over time I had a good relationship with Bradford, and the people who were recruited to run the oligo synthesis program at Antisense Therapeutics. We had many convivial dinners and many intense conversations and discussions. But, eventually I realized that Bradford had his own agenda. He was not only interested in antisense, he started another research program involving the work of a famous cancer expert he had met while at the pharmaceutical company. They had apparently turned down his proposed research program with them, and Bradford had now persuaded Wally and others that he should go ahead and do this too. As time went on he gradually phased down the antisense project in favor of his own preferred project.

I approached Wally and asked him what could be done, after all the business plan that we had written did not explicitly include this new project. But, he and others advised me that the business plan was only a rough guide and after some time could be neglected. Also, once Bradford was CEO he could basically do what he liked as long as the Board went along with it. So far he had persuaded them that his project had a greater chance of success than antisense. So I saw the company was being stolen away from under my nose. Even with legal advice it seemed there was nothing I could do about it. But, I had learned a hell of a lot about venture capital and starting a company and I had learned that most of those in the business played hard-ball.

14. The falling out

For several months things seemed to be going well. I was busy conferring with the six post-docs and two technicians now working in my lab, and then going to NJ once a month. I took the train to Metro Center and a car met me there and then took me back later, and sometimes I flew to Newark and back. But, also I was busy writing up scientific papers for publication as well as reading the scientific literature in an effort to keep up with the fast moving pace of research.

Every few days I met with each post-doc when he had some results to go over and we would discuss them and then agree on a plan for the next stage of the research. Also, we discussed any pertinent papers that had been published on the subject. Then monthly, we had a seminar meeting where each one in turn presented the results of their project. We also had a monthly Branch meeting where someone from the Branch would present his/her research.

Then one day my technician Paul Laguno asked to see me and unusually he closed the sliding door to my room. What could be so private that he needed to do this? What he told me was very disturbing,

"I didn't know whether to tell you this or not, but Sam has not been doing his own work, he has been ordering Leila and Matsuo about and getting them to do his work. I told Leila to tell you, but she was scared to come to you because she didn't want to get Sam in trouble and she is scared of him. Also, you may have noticed that Matsuo is hardly ever around, he now works only a night when Sam is not around, so that he can work without his interference."

"How long has this been going on?" I asked. "About 3 months," he answered.

I was shocked and very upset. I had noticed that Sam was not often working in the lab, but he usually had some results to report, on oligos synthesized and experiments done. I had arranged collaborations with several other researchers, in NIH and outside, where we would supply the PS oligos to test their particular target gene. It was very important to carefully choose a specific cancer gene target to test the antisense oligo method against cancer, and we did this with a colleague in the NCI. We obtained positive results compared to PO oligo controls, and this had been Sam's project. However, no one had complained to me about him and obviously he had been careful to cover this up.

I spoke to Leila and she reluctantly confirmed what Paul had told me. I also tried to speak to Matsuo the Japanese post-doc, but he remained typically abstruse. But, after speaking with him about the problem and getting nowhere I had a visit from Sam's post-doc, Kaito, who approached me on behalf of Matsuo, so I supposed this was the way it was done, the more senior Japanese was his representative. He complained to me in no uncertain terms that Matsuo would not take orders from Sam, and I must do something about this. I assured him that I would.

Sam had taken to calling me at home in the evening around dinner time, to tell me the latest scuttlebutt in the lab. I supposed he thought I would be grateful to him, but I basically just listened. On several occasions I had been to the lab late in the evening to check on an experiment, and I had found Sam sitting in the secretary's chair going through the flimsy copies of the letters that had been sent out that day that she kept in a ring file. At first this didn't particularly alarm me, but later I realized that he was keeping tabs on everything that was going on in the lab.

When I heard about his exploiting the other members of the synthesis lab I decided belatedly to check up on his previous background at NCI. I spoke to a colleague who was another Section Head in the Pharmacology Branch, and he told me that Ace had first requested that he take Sam in, and he had refused because he knew of his reputation. I knew Sam had been in the Medicine Branch before, but then I learnt that he had also been in the Pediatric Oncology branch. The Head of that Brach was a particularly nice fellow who I had met several times, so I went to see him. What I heard from him was very worrying. It seems he had thrown Sam out of his Branch for being lazy and obstreperous.

Then I went to see Mort Feldman Head of the Medicine Branch and he told me a similar story, that he had allowed Sam into his Branch on a temporary basis and after a few days had asked him to leave. It turned out that I was Sam's last chance at NIH, and Ace had sicked him on me without reporting this background, I had been the patsy, and it was mainly because I was not in the clinical service and I was not privy to all this background.

I decided to confront Sam about this whole situation. I chose a time when no-one else was around before leaving work. I stayed on a bit later on a day when he was still there. I called him into my little office and said, "I have discovered that you have been ordering Leila and Matsuo around, but they resent this and it has to stop! I gave you a memo when you started here describing the work you have to do and you are not doing it." I was not prepared for his reaction, he became very angry and red-faced and he came right up to me as if restraining himself with his arms held back and he threatened me. He said, "you can't talk to me like that, I'm an oncologist here and what are you, and if I say so Ace is going to give me your lab and get rid of you, you're nothing."

I was completely taken aback by this aggressive behavior, nothing like this had ever happened to me before. Nevertheless, I held my cool and I said to him, "back off, who do you think you are, you don't have tenure here and this is my lab, I want to you out of my lab, as soon as possible. I am giving you a month's notice, or whatever the minimum is. I know I was your last chance to make good here at NCI and you screwed up again, so now you're finished, get out." And we stood there glaring at each other. Then he said, "You'll hear more about this, I'm going to Ace to complain that you are incompetent and preventing me from doing my work and I'm going to see my lawyer and I'm going to sue your ass, you scumbag!" And with that he turned and marched out of the room.

I sat down and immediately wrote a memo to Ace telling him about the problems with Sam, his exploitation of the others in the lab, his tendency to exaggerate his contributions (that I documented) and his abrasiveness, and I wanted him out of my lab at the earliest possible time. I left this on Ace's desk the next morning and when he had read it he called me in. He tried to be diplomatic, but I would not accept it, reminding him of Sam's background that he had not told me about. So he reluctantly agreed to remove Sam from my lab and set him up in another lab. But, what I realized was that Ace was more or less siding with Sam. If he was going to set him up in another lab, what work would he be doing, if not the same work he had been doing in my lab, but now with Ace himself.

The following days were difficult with Sam moving his stuff out of my lab, and I realized that I had to make sure he did not take anything that belonged to me. But, this was touchy because he could appeal over my head to Ace and after all most of it didn't belong to me personally but rather to the Branch and the Institute. However, on one subject I was adamant. Sam could not take any of the oligos that Leila had synthesized, since he had not done any of the syntheses himself. He also had no access to the DNA synthesizer, so if he wanted to duplicate our work he would have to find another synthesizer, because I would not let him have access to mine. And Ace had no control over it, because it had been bought with AIDS money, not Branch money.

I gave orders to everyone in the lab, and particularly Leila, that Sam was not allowed to take anything else out of the lab, specifically not oligos from the freezer.

It was at this point that Walter Hazen, my pediatrician post-doc, who was preparing to leave the lab to take a position in Philadelphia told me something unsettling. He said that Sam had sworn him to secrecy some three months before and told him that Ace was preparing to get rid of me and promote him in my place. I asked him why he had not warned me of this conversation before, and he simply shrugged and decent fellow that he was said," but, I agreed to keep it secret." Maybe that was also a warning to him and that was why he was leaving.

15. Leila Subramanian

The phone rang exactly at dinner-time, about 6 pm, just as I was sitting down to eat. As I picked up the phone I thought to myself "Oh, not again." but this time the voice on the other end was female, it was Leila Subramanian, my technician. She said "I hope it's all right to call you now," and I detected a note of panic in her voice. "What's wrong?" I asked. I could tell from the tone of her voice that she had been crying.

"It's just that I'm afraid," she said. "Why?" I asked. "Well, it's just that Sam has been in the lab and tried to take stuff from the fridge and I told him he couldn't, and then he threatened me, but I told him to leave and then I locked the lab door, and I'm frightened because he's outside waiting, and he is angry, and I'm afraid to leave."

"Don't worry, you did the right thing calling me, what did he say to you?"

"He said, you're a 40 pound girl and I'm a 140 pound guy, and if you don't let me take what I want you will regret it!" Her voice sounded teary, and I could tell that she was afraid.

I asked "is he still there?" "Yes," she replied. "Well, this is what you should do, hang up and call the NIH police, there's always someone on duty at the entrance, call them, the number is in the telephone directory or it may be directly on the phone you are using, and tell them that a man is threatening you and ask them to come to escort you from the building. Meanwhile I'm coming right over, I'll be there in about 10 minutes, I'll meet you at the entrance." "OK," she replied and we hung up.

I immediately put my coat on and ran to my car and raced over to NIH. I screeched to a halt outside the entrance and Leila was there with a policeman. She was a diminutive figure beside him. Her eyes were red from crying and she was obviously upset. I asked her what had happened after we hung up, and she said that Sam had left as soon as she called the police, he could hear her through the door, and when the policeman came he was nowhere to be seen. The policeman asked me what he should do, and I told him that for now all was OK, but I asked him to make sure that he wrote a report of what had happened and he assured me he would. So Leila went with him into their little office by the entrance and gave him a statement. I also told him what she had told me while we were on the phone. This time it seemed that Sam had gone too far!

16. The Grievance hearing

Although Sam Schwartz had been the aggressor he had neatly turned the tables on me by accusing me in writing of trying to destroy his career and by bringing Ace Ericson in on his side. A formal grievance hearing was called by Arthur Grosz, who was the head of Radiation Oncology and was the acting head of the Division at that time. I looked forward to this meeting with dread. I knew Arthur through my other work with MRI and I had always found him a decent fellow to get along with. I hoped he too harbored no ill will towards me.

I entered the Director's conference room at the appointed time, and found the others already there. Arthur sat at the head of the table, Sam and Ace sat on one side and I sat opposite them. Arthur opened the meeting with a formal statement that this was a grievance action being brought against me by my former student Sam Schwartz. He asked Schwartz to enumerate the particulars.

Schwartz then went into a diatribe against me, how I had mistreated him, how I had thrown him out of my lab, how I had refused to give him access to my lab when he had valuable products that he had made and stored in my refrigerator. Finally, he accused me of trying to destroy his career. He said that I had written defamatory letters about him to our collaborators, and he happened to have an example of such a letter that had been given to him by one of them. Whereupon, he produced a piece of paper and flung it unceremoniously across the table at Arthur Grosz.

As Arthur picked up this letter he asked me if I had anything to say in my defense. I replied that I had never tried to ruin his career, that the letter was basically innocuous, telling people that he was no longer in my lab, and that he had behaved so badly that I had no alternative except to ask him to leave my lab. At this point Arthur scanned the letter, then read it aloud. It was short and to the point, it merely said that Sam Schwartz was leaving my lab and in future the recipient should make contact directly with me. Arthur said "there's nothing defamatory in this letter, I don't know what you're making such a fuss about," and he threw the letter back to Sam in a dismissive manner.

Whereupon, seeing that Arthur Grosz was not so sympathetic to their cause, Ace stepped in. He declared in no uncertain terms that I had mistreated Sam Schwartz, that as far as he was concerned I was the miscreant, and he certainly felt that I was trying to harm Sam's career. Then Arthur turned to me to give me a chance to respond to these accusations.

 I pointed out that I had taken Sam into my lab at Ace's request as every other post-doc. I had given him a project to carry out and I had documentation to prove it. But, from the beginning Schwartz had been lazy and manipulative. He did not do the work he was assigned, but spent his time ordering others to do it for him, specifically my technician Leila, and he had conspired with Ace Ericson to take over my antisense project. I did not know if it was because Ace wanted my position or because he was jealous of the success of this project, but there was no doubt, as shown by their performance today, that they were in this together to get me.

Furthermore, I added that in fact this should be a meeting to discuss the disgusting behavior of Sam Schwartz towards Leila Subramanian. I recounted that occurrence, and said that Leila should have been here to confront Sam, but she had taken a few days off and was afraid to be near him. However, she had issued a grievance against Sam that preceded his against me, and his action was evidently intended to subvert that.

After listening to all of us, Arthur said in summary, that he saw no evidence that I was trying to destroy Schwartz's career, but on the contrary it was clear that Schwartz and Ace were ganging up on me, although he wasn't sure why. He ordered us to stay apart and to stop this bickering, and he said he would interview Leila to see what her description of her experience was. Then he would make a final written determination.

So although it was a terrible experience to go through, and none of my previous 30 or so post-docs had ever treated me in such a way, at least so far I had come out unscathed and Arthur Grosz seemed fair and if anything leaning in my direction.

A few days later Leila came in and met with Arthur Grosz. The outcome was that Arthur summoned Sam Schwartz to a meeting in Ericson's office and after asking each of them several questions he decided that Sam had behaved badly, had inappropriately threatened Leila and consequently he had to apologize to her in front of himself and Ericson. Obviously Sam was very chagrined at having to apologize to Leila in this way. He had gambled and lost.

Several people, including myself were standing outside the office waiting to hear the verdict. Sam came out first and without saying anything, his face bright red, and seeing the waste-basket before him, kicked it with strength. Its contents flew out all over the floor, but he stepped over the mess and disappeared down the corridor. We laughed at his predicament.

After speaking to Leila and reviewing her grievance against Schwartz, Arthur Grosz wrote us a letter detailing his decision. He concluded that there was no case to make regarding any attempt on my part to ruin Schwartz's career, but on the contrary, for reasons not fully clear, Ericson and Schwartz had connived together against me, and probably with the intention of forcing me to leave. He said this behavior was unacceptable and must stop immediately, otherwise he would be forced to take more punitive action. I was vindicated, but the atmosphere was such that I had no alternative but to look for a position elsewhere. I could not continue working under someone who was clearly using any tactics to get rid of me.

Later I heard that Sam was threatening to sue me and someone else in civil court, so I approached the Legal Advisor at NIH and asked for his advice and he told me that an NIH employee could not sue another employee for anything said or done in pursuance (that was how he spoke) of his government work. Since I was required to ensure a smoothly operating laboratory and since I had been required to give my opinion about Sam, then there was no case. In addition, since Sam was a post-doc and not a permanent employee like me, he had no status to sue. Well, that was a relief to me.

17. Sabotage

One way in which Ace's hostility towards me was manifest was that he ordered me not to use any of his labs for my work, and this included the use of equipment in them.

Leila was doing a project for me to test the amount of terminal hydroxyl group on the end of the oligos. In order to do this one treated the synthetic oligo with radioactive 32P-phosphate using a specific enzyme that added the phosphate group to the free hydroxyl end. By knowing how much oligo was used and how much radiation became tagged to it, one could work out how good the synthesis was. Leila had already started this experiment. In order to determine the amount of radioactive material that was tagged one used a piece of equipment that was on another floor that was used by many different groups in the lab. Leila came to me and asked if it was OK for her to use this particular piece of equipment and I said we had no choice, it's the only one that can measure the amount of radioactivity coming off the column in the position of the tagged oligo.

So she set up the column on the apparatus with the radioactivity counter. Later she told me that while she was doing this she noted that Sam was prowling around and walked by the room several times. But, she ignored him and continued with the experiment. Then she had to leave the column to run for some time and she left it alone.

When she came back several hours later she found that someone had changed the settings on the apparatus, so that the experiment had run through much too quickly and the result could not be determined. What was most worrisome and dangerous was that the 32P labeled material had been allowed to drip onto the apparatus itself and had contaminated it. It was clear that this was a case of deliberate sabotage.

I went to see Ace and told him what had happened. He told me that Sam had complained to him that we were using Branch lab equipment against his order (it was not actually his equipment) and he, Ace, had told him to warn us. Apparently, instead Sam had taken matters into his own hands.

I decided this was too much, so I made an appointment with Brian Cranmer, the Chief of the NCI and when I got to see him I told him what had happened. Not only was it completely unacceptable to sabotage someone else's scientific experiment, but in this case also there was radioactivity involved and the outcome could be very dangerous. Now there would have to be a test of the radioactivity spill and a clean-up. Not only that, the experiment was ruined and would have to be repeated.

Sam was called in by Cranmer and was given a final ultimatum. He was told that he would have to leave NCI at the end of his current annual fellowship. He had several months to find another suitable job.

18. The CIA

One morning soon after I arrived at the lab I received a call from a woman who asked if she could visit me to discuss antisense. I asked her who she represented and she said she would explain when she saw me. After I said Ok, she asked if she could come then and she said she was in the building and could come right up. So I agreed.

When she came in I was surprised to see that she was Asian. She introduced herself and gave me her card. She was well-dressed, smart and I guessed around 40 years of age. She had an American accent without a trace of foreign accent. She said that she had seen some of my publications on antisense and she told me that she wished to speak to me confidentially. I asked her why and she replied that she worked for the CIA!

They were trying to assess the potential of antisense, and she asked me to swear secrecy. I agreed, but asked her why the CIA would be interested in antisense. She said she had heard of some work on antisense related to behavioral effects. I told her that I knew about some work on mouse mutants whose behavior (chasing their tail) had been altered by an antisense oligo, but it was published in the open scientific literature. She said she knew about my recent visit to the Soviet Union for a conference on antisense and she wondered if I had heard of any Soviet work on this topic. I told her that I was a loyal American and that I would give her any such information if I had seen any, but I would not spy on my scientific colleagues. She seemed satisfied by that and asked me to call her if anything new came up.

A few days later I received a call from a man who mentioned this meeting and who asked me to meet him at a mutually agreeable time at a particular bar called "1789," that is in Georgetown near the Georgetown University campus. It is always full of students and always crowded, so a great place to meet.

When I got there I was met at the entrance by this man, who was not remarkable in any way. He did wear a large beige raincoat that might have been a "trench-coat" but I wasn't sure. He was very friendly and chatty and then started asking me questions about the trip to the USSR. We ordered beers and then he zipped open a small leather case with a thick notebook inside, and began to write notes. He became more and more detailed in his questions, asking me about the people we met in the Soviet Union, their demeanor, their conversations, their interests. But, it became too noisy to really hear well, with all the jocks in football jerseys, so we decided to leave. We walked over to the Georgetown University gym and past there to the steep stairs that led down towards the bridge across the Potomac River (the same stairs featured in the movie "The Exorcist"). He wanted to descend, but I said that I had had enough and I wanted to leave. We shook hands and I agreed to meet him again.

In a way I was disappointed, this was nothing like what I had expected, there was no scientific content in this interrogation. He wanted to know about the people, the Russians and visitors and their interactions. In other words it was spying on them, precisely what I had said I didn't want to do. When he called me a few days later, I told him about my reluctance, I said that I did not want to tell him about the people involved. He said OK, if I wanted to talk about the science, that was OK by him, and he asked me to meet him where we had separated last time, at the top of those stairs.

When I met him it was cold day, and the wind was particularly strong at the top of the stairs. In a flash I imagined he wanted to push me down the stairs (as in the movie) but I resisted the fear. As it turned out we went to have lunch at the Indian restaurant a few blocks away on the main M Street. Over japatis and ghosht he asked me what I thought was the Soviet interest in antisense and whether or not there was any evidence of their work on behavioral experiments. I told him that their interest seemed to be purely scientific, in other words here was a new area of science, with great potential applications in medicine, and they were interested in learning as much as they could from us. I saw or heard no evidence of behavioral work, but that could have been deliberate on their part. I also told him that I could quite easily pick out the KGB or Soviet minders, who were there to watch and check on what was said, since they had no scientific credentials and I gave him the names that they went under and their descriptions (I even had some photos). But, then I told him that that was all I had to tell him and I didn't want to meet him any more to continue this exchange. We discussed my reasons for a while, but at the end of the meal I said goodbye and left. So ended my brief flirtation with the CIA.

19. Leaving NCI

I had also decided that I had to leave Ace's lab and my first recourse was to look elsewhere in NCI. I had several meetings with the Head of the Institute, Brian Cranmer, in his plush office on the top floor of the administration building. But this failed to produce any result. As a member of his staff told me confidentially, his management style was to allow matters to fester until a solution arose naturally. He was not going to help me.

The previous Institute Head, Vance La Lotta, was now at Sloan-Kettering in NY and I went up there and had an excellent interview with him in his even plushier office. He offered me a great set-up with a whole new large lab of my own. But, then it transpired that the lab was still being built, and that Vance had political problems of his own. It seemed that people there were conspiring against him and I was viewed as one of his plants. The Head of Pharmacology there basically opposed my appointment, while pretending to support it, and the whole thing was a political nightmare.

I called Mort Feldman who had been the Head of the Medicine Branch in NCI before he left a few months previously to head up the Lombardi Cancer Center in Georgetown University Medical School. Mort knew all about Sam Schwartz, because he had thrown him out of his lab before I foolishly took him into mine at Ace's urging. When I told him what had happened to me, he was very sympathetic and asked me to go over there for an interview. I met with him and the Head of Pharmacology, Ronald Wooten, and they both said they were enthusiastic to have me.

Wooten was quite new to the job and had received funds to establish a Cancer Pharmacology group (he was in cardiology himself), and I fitted right into that. So it was agreed that I would move there with funds from the company Antisense Therapeutics that I had helped found and had an agreement with. It seemed that nothing was available unless you were bringing money in.

Someone told me that a Medical School is like a whore house, they rent you a room and you have to supply them with funds, and they don't particularly care how you get them. So I made a deal to leave NCI and go to Georgetown Medical School, located in the salubrious district of Georgetown not far away in Washington DC. I would be better off both in terms of income and research funds than I was in the government lab, but on the other hand there was no employment guarantee as there was in the government. To get tenure would take several years and I could be out on my ear if I failed to keep the funds rolling in. Nevertheless, it was a good prospect and so I left the security of the NIH where I had worked for 22 years and moved to Georgetown Medical School, where I became a Full Professor.

I left NCI in 1990 with regret, but maybe I should have stayed and toughed it out. Because within a year they managed to find a really good Head of the Medicine

Branch and Ace was asked to leave. He simply was not up to the job. Then again, things change and it's best to go with the flow. At Georgetown I was in for another of life's unpredictable adventures.

20. Georgetown

Things worked out very well at Georgetown, I was busy continuing my antisense research. I had managed to take a few of the post-docs with me, based on their current status, since it was considered inappropriate to cut them off in the middle of their projects. I had funds from two sources, from an agreement with the antisense company Antisense Therapeutics to support my research, it seemed that Bradford Singer was prepared to be generous as long as I left him alone, and from the money that had been donated to Georgetown for the formation of the Cancer Pharmacology group, of which I was to receive $350,000. I was advised by Wooten to use the Antisense Therapeutics money first and leave the other in the account at Georgetown as a back-up for when I needed it.

While I was at Georgetown a big scandal occurred. The Cancer Center in Georgetown Medical School was named after Vince Lombardi, the former great football coach, "the winningest coach in history" as he was known. He had died of cancer in Georgetown Medical School when he was the coach of the Washington Redskins. As a result the Cancer Center was not only named after him, but the NFL provided funds to support the Center's research programs thru large donations, partly from the dinner held every year in Washington which most of the NFL players attended.

Mort Feldman was a very aggressive researcher and well-known expert in breast cancer and set about reinstating the high level of prestige of that Center. In order to do this he decided that Georgetown needed a new research building to house the new Cancer Center. The Dean of the Medical School agreed and arranged for a well-known Italian Pharmaceutical company to provide funds to cover the largest part of the cost of this building, amounting to hundreds of millions of dollars. Georgetown had a close relationship with this company because it was of course a Catholic University and had many dealings with the Church and State in Italy.

However, during the building of this research center, the Italian pharmaceutical company went broke, and overnight the construction stopped. Then there were discussions held within the administration of the medical school, whether or not to continue with the building without a replacement sponsor. The Dean and Mort, the Head of the Cancer Center, decided to go ahead, with the total cost being supported by the Medical School alone.

The building when it was finally finished was opened with a grand ceremony and great fanfare and was a wonderful addition to the research facilities at Georgetown. But, because of the extra costs, all the Medical School budgets had to be slashed and all the Departments understandably had their budgets cut by ca. 30%. It also led to the firing of the Dean of the Medical School.

One day when I decided to use some of the money in my account at Georgetown, I was told by Wooten's administrator that there was no money left in the account. When I questioned this, she advised me not to raise the matter with Wooten. I went to the Dean of research at Georgetown Med to get his advice and he told me "you can't simply let Wooten steal money that has been allocated to you as part of your agreement to come here."

So I made an appointment to see Wooten and confronted him with the loss of my funds. He admitted that he had used them to cover the deficit of the Department, and that he would make good on them, but not right away, within the next few years. I accepted this, I had no other choice, and I must admit that he made good on his promise. But, he was never friendly towards me after that, and I realized that I had to give up any hope of getting his support to apply for tenure.

Meanwhile the early promise of antisense was fading in the face of many difficulties, including the cost of production of oligos, the difficulty in cell uptake and then inconclusive *in vivo* tests. So I gave up my faith in the Medical School system, gave up research on antisense and left for another of life's adventures.

Overall I can say that antisense was good to me, and it lasted for a few years. I still haven't given up my hope that indeed genetic drugs will one day replace the harsh toxic agents used for cancer chemotherapy, but I am no longer actively involved in that endeavor. Some 40 antisense drugs have been developed and two antisense oligos have indeed been approved by the FDA, one for use in a topical (local) anti-cancer application. I hope another generation of researchers will look again at the potential of PS-oligos as drugs against genetically based diseases. If so, I will be glad to have played a small role in the development of this concept. It was not always easy but it was quite a venture. I console myself with the belief that it is only capable and successful people who instill in others the need to subvert and supplant.

~~~~~~~~~~~~~~~

Postscript: In writing this account of an actual research project and the human interactions involved, I have been forced to leave out many complications that arose during the process. Notably, the interactions with many other colleagues, both cooperative and hostile and I have had to simplify certain events. However, in doing so, I have endeavored to retain the essence of any event that I personally experienced. Names have been changed to protect the innocent. Only by trying to write these events down is one forced to confront the complexity of human behavior.

21. Glossary

Antisense: The sequence of bases in the complementary strand of DNA that do not code for a protein product (see sense)

Atom: The smallest unit of chemical matter, a unit of an element

ATP: Adenosine tri-phosphate, the energy-containing substance in the cell and body

Base pairing: The combination of two bases into specific pairs, A with T and G with C. This was discovered by Erwin Chargaff in the 1950's and was used by Watson and Crick to help determine the *double* helical structure of DNA

Base: a nitrogenous substance, four of which are commonly found in DNA, adenine (A), thymine (T), guanine (G) and cytidine (C)

Deoxyribose: The sugar (carbohydrate) component of DNA

DNA: Abbreviation for deoxyribonucleic acid, a substance found in the nucleus of the cell that is the genetic substance.

DNA Synthesizer: A machine in which individual nucleotides are added one at a time automatically to a chain to form an oligonucleotide

Drug: A substance that when taken into the body causes a specific physiological effect

Messenger RNA: Written as mRNA, the nucleic acid that takes the genetic information from the DNA in the nucleus into the cell to be expressed into protein.

Molecule: A group of atoms bonded together in a specific way

Nucleotide: The chemical unit of DNA consisting of a base, a sugar (deoxyribose) and a phosphate group

Oligo: shortened form of oliogonucleotide, a small piece of synthetic DNA with a specific sequence of bases used as a drug to down-regulate the expression of a selected gene

Phosphate: A chemical group containing a phosphorus atom bound to four oxygen atoms (abbrev. to PO)

Phosphonate: A chemically modified phosphate group with a carbon atom in place of one of the oxygen atoms (abbrev. to PM)

Phosphorothioate: A chemically modified phosphate group with a sulfur atom in place of one of the oxygen atoms (abbrev. to PS)

Post-doc: A post-doctoral fellow, who already has a PhD degree and is learning how to do research supported by a fellowship

RNA: ribonucleic acid, a nucleic acid that contains the sugar component ribose

Sense: The sequence of bases in DNA and its messenger RNA that code for a protein product

Sugar: a substance, also named a carbohydrate, with atoms of carbon, oxygen and hydrogen

Ulpan

Murder at Green Beach

I Green Beach

The road south from Netanya passes through Poleg, and then narrows and turns left as it reaches the shore. Before you is a magnificent view of Green Beach, desolate and alluring. The white-crested waves ride in stately procession endlessly to the beach. The sun shines brilliantly and the wind whips the sand into sudden whorls. To the south is a headland criss-crossed by sandy paths, and on its top sits the Wingate Institute for sports and athletics. Beyond that the beach stretches far into the distance. In the curve of the shoreline sits the Green Beach Hotel, isolated from the rest of the world.

To the right an unpaved road leads directly down onto the beach, with a weathered sign for a restaurant "Pundak Hayam" in English and Hebrew, meaning "fruits of the sea." The road itself veers to the left, and there is the entrance to the Green Beach Hotel. It is a somewhat dilapidated but charming hotel, where tourist buses disgorge overnighters on their trips around Israel.

Inside the gate of the Green Beach Hotel, to the left of the parking lot, beyond the main building, are a series of cottages and huts. Between them one emerges onto a small compound with signs indicating that this is the Green Beach Ulpan. This is one of the schools for the intensive study of the Hebrew language, an ulpan. Since Israel has had to absorb in a short time millions of immigrants from many countries speaking different languages, they had to devise an efficient way of teaching them all their new language, Hebrew. In the Ulpan everything is taught in Hebrew, and generally new immigrants get a free five month course to prepare them for their new life in Israel, courtesy of the Israeli Ministry of Absorption (*Misrad Haklita*). The Ulpan also takes many students from abroad.

Everything at the Ulpan looks dilapidated, and the signs are weather-beaten. A forlorn plaster camel sits in the middle of the grass patch. The lessons are given in the huts and concrete building scattered around. Further away, towards the sea, in the rows of low buildings are the rooms of the residents who have come from all around the world to learn Hebrew and to enjoy a stimulating experience. A sign says "Welcome" in many languages, "Shalom, Bienvenue, Dasvedaniye, Welkommen." As the instructor said, "Welcome to the Green Beach Ulpan where we will spend the next few months learning Hebrew, getting to know each other, and sharing interesting experiences."

II The Ulpan

What seems like hundreds of people are milling around in aimless patterns. There are written signs in several languages, but no-one takes any notice of them. Asking directions in English sometimes gets puzzled responses in Russian. Finally people congregate in one large room, and take seats randomly at several tables. They glance self-consciously at each other. Those who had graduated from the previous class and are continuing exchange confident comments.

The Director, a woman in her fifties, arrives and gives a pep talk in Hebrew and English, followed by a translation in Russian, to accommodate the many immigrants from the former Soviet Union. A hubbub of translations in other languages, notably French and Arabic, also occur. This is like the tower of Babel itself.

It becomes apparent that when their table number is called each student will present themselves in the adjoining room and wait on line. Papers are checked and payments are made. Then a registration package is collected which contains final instructions. After the paperwork is completed each student is then sent to a classroom to be tested by a teacher, and then assigned to a particular level of study. There are five levels, *aleph, bet1, bet2, gimel and daled*, but because of the many beginners there are two *aleph* classes in which they teach the alphabet and the basics.

After a while the groups reform and tea and coffee is served. Then there are other instructions in many languages. Those who are residents break off and go to be assigned rooms by the hotel. Luggage is hauled. In the middle people arrive carrying backpacks and have to be given instructions in German or Turkish.

Neil looked around. This was an incredible mixture of people, just what he liked. Being an international reporter from Australia this was his element. But being Jewish, he had become tired of making excuses for himself all around the world. He was fed up with being harangued in Arabic and thrown out of press conferences in Indonesia. He was annoyed with lame excuses in Karachi and Kuala Lumpur. He had decided that Israel existed, and so he came to learn Hebrew in 1997 and to see if he could hack it here for a while.

The rest of the crowd had their own reasons for being there. He had signed up for three months. Unlike the immigrants it was costing him. But, if he liked it he could become an immigrant later. The room was filled with old and young, men and women, white and black. He noticed a beautiful blond girl, must get in her class. He did not want to speak English and mix with Americans and Brits, but it was inevitable.

He heard a familiar accent, "where are you from?.." In quick succession he met an older guy named Jeff who came from California, and was now here to see what it was like in Israel, a young woman who was not very communicative from Baltimore, and a young man from New Jersey named Hugo. As they mingled he heard others speaking English. After he got his room he decided that he would check out all the English speakers. If he was going to have a good time he had to start there.

III The Bodies

Two months later a call was made to the police in Netanya.
"Go to Pundak Hayam at Green Beach. Someone is dead."
Then they rang off. It was a man, who spoke heavily Russian-accented Hebrew.

No recordings were then made of routine calls. From this you might conclude that there is little crime in Netanya. But, you would be wrong, since Netanya has emerged as a center for crime in Israel. It is rumored that the Russian mafia has its headquarters there. About 20% of the population consists of Russian immigrants, higher than the national average, and speaking Russian is not a limitation. There is a joke, "what is the third language in Netanya," answer "Hebrew," the second is French. The ulpan teacher joked, "what is it with all you Russians, do they give you all *peteks* (chits) saying 'go to Netanya.'"

There have been several gang-related murders in Netanya. It's not up to the level of Naples or Boston, but it happens. On May 26, 1997, Alex Dubitsky, a small time crook and gambler was murdered in broad daylight in the center of Netanya. He was seated at a popular outdoor cafe. A motorcyclist on a light motorcycle rode up to him, got off, circled him twice, and then shot him twice in the head. The assassin calmly remounted his motorcycle and rode away. No-one saw his face because he did not remove his helmet. It was a professional hit.

So one should not be fooled by the calm exterior of Netanya, a quiet holiday resort and retirement town. Underneath there is a battle for the gambling, prostitution and crime rackets that are developing here. This is by way of background, so that when the police in Netanya received a call in Russian-accented Hebrew about a body in the area, they were not very surprised. They assumed it was just another gang-land hit, with the body stashed in an out-of-the way place down on Green Beach. In their usual fashion they thought about the call for a while, and after about 30 min decided to go and investigate.

Two police cars drove down the deserted beach road towards the restaurant. They parked in the back, and walked around looking for a way in. Out of season the restaurant was closed and all the doors had been locked and covered against break-ins. Someone found a door on the side that had been broken open. The scene that greeted them when they walked into the main room was one of terrible carnage.

In the dark, with shafts of bright sunlight streaking in through holes, they could make out on a table in the middle of the room the nude body of a young woman. She was tied down to the table at the four corners by her hands and feet. Her body was covered in congealed blood. Before her death she had suffered terribly. There was blood spattered around the table. Her blond hair shone brilliantly in a shaft of sunlight. Lying nearby on the floor in a pool of blood was the body of a young man.

All hell broke loose; soon dozens of police cars were making the trek to the restaurant out on the beach. The police chief decided that they needed help from Police HQ in Jerusalem, and the best fingerprint and homicide detectives were sent down to Netanya to assist the locals. The case was placed into the hands of Detective Shlomo Ben-Artzi, experienced in the methods of the Netanya underworld. He had difficulty keeping the crowd of cops from trampling all over the crime scene. Photographs, blood and other samples were taken for lab analysis.

Standing in the fresh breeze from the sea, recovering from the stench inside, and looking out from the restaurant, the nearest inhabited place was the Green Beach Hotel, and the Ulpan there. Shlomo made the decision to interview everyone who worked at the hotel, and especially the Ulpan.

IV Elizaveta

After settling in, and finding the room hardly big enough to swing a cat, he went out for the tea break. A chance to socialize and meet people.

There were basically two groups of people attending the Ulpan, those who were residents at the Hotel and those who came in daily from Netanya. The former were mainly a mixture of people from around the world who wanted for one reason or another to learn Hebrew. The latter were overwhelmingly Russian-speaking. His natural place was with the former group, but he decided to make a point of trying to make contacts with the Russian locals. They needed to learn Hebrew to live and work in Israel. Through them Neil could find out what Israel was really like, and also learn to find his way around the city.

Between lessons, people congregated and chatted over cups of tea and coffee. "Where are you from?" Details were exchanged, addresses and phone numbers written down, discrete flirting took place. Jobs and apartments were being sought, rents were discussed and advice given, in all languages, Russian, French, English, German and Hebrew.

Through this crowd, he saw her. She was beautiful, she stood out, she had short blonde hair and her features were perfect. She was slim and sculpted, she was amazing. He was drawn to her, as evidently so were other men. As he approached he heard her talking in Russian to a knot of young men, she saw him and returned his gaze. Just as he was about to turn away she came over to him and said "You speak English, so do I."

He was surprised. She uttered a throaty laugh at his response.

"I didn't expect you would speak English," he said "Yes, I learnt it at school in Russia"

"What is your name?"

"Elizaveta."

"Where are you from in Russia?" "From Kavkaz." As they spoke he stared intently at her face, like that of an angel, he thought. Just at that instant the sun was behind her and caught her hair making the appearance of a halo. He was transfixed.

He told her about himself, his long journey around the world, to find what? Himself? Then they agreed to talk again and when the bell rang they went back to their class as if nothing had happened.

Next time they met he asked her about herself, she seemed eager to tell him. Her father was Jewish and wanted to get out, her mother was Russian and did not want to leave. She wanted to get away from Kavkaz, in the Caucasus region. It was remote and boring. She had come with her father, and now lived in Israel, in Netanya. These chats were more intense than they might have been, maybe it was his journalistic skills, or maybe something more, but he felt he wanted to know more about Elizaveta. She gave him her telephone number at home.

After the afternoon session of Ulpan ended he offered her a lift and she readily accepted. He had rented a car so he could get back and forth into town easily, it was about a 15 min drive. In the car they spoke together with ease. She told him that life was difficult for her, and then she stopped as if deciding whether or not to tell a secret and then she spoke softly and intensely. She said "My father abuses me."

He was taken aback, not quite knowing how to react to this disturbing information.
"How does he abuse you, does he beat you?"
"No," she replied conspiratorily, "he uses me, like a wife."
As he drove he tried to decide what to make of this unsettling information. What could he do about it, or what should he do? He saw no way, he certainly could not confront the father, who in any case would deny it. He could not go to the police, how could he explain this to them. As they reached near where she wanted to get off, he slowed down and she leaned across and kissed him on the lips. A surge of adrenaline shot through him. She smiled at him and jumped out of the car.
The thought went through his mind "damaged goods."

V The Dunes

One day just before class Hugo from New Jersey collared him and said, "Jeff is taking us for a ride in the dunes, he rented a dune buggy, and he wants you to come."

"But, what about class?" he said. "Forget about it," he intoned in his NJ accent.

Then he added, "He invited Elizaveta, that cute blond, and she won't come unless you do." He was confused, but decided what the hell, might as well have some fun.

He climbed into the front seat of the buggy next to Jeff. He was a distinguished looking man, obviously wealthy and confident. Hugo sat next to Elizaveta in the back. As we started to traverse the dunes, the buggy went up and down like a roller-coaster. Elizaveta grabbed on to Hugo and said, "This turns me on." She also grabbed hold of his hand on the back of the front seat. He left it there, then saw that she and Hugo were embracing and he pulled it away. Before long they were going at it in the back seat, and soon were having sex. He was embarrassed, but tried to pretend it was alright.

After a while, when he supposed they were finished, Jeff stopped the buggy hopped out and climbed into the back seat while Hugo replaced him at the wheel. Then as we took off he saw that Jeff was kissing Elizaveta and then having sex with her. He was furious, not only because she was obviously a nymphomaniac, but that it was not him, he was jealous. Hugo turned to me and said, "your turn next." But, he couldn't take it, he said "stop here," and he jumped down and started to trudge back to the Hotel through the sand. Hugo looked surprised, but he could never have sex with a girl after others had already done it. It put him off, he had scruples.

Later he watched as they returned to the car park. When they got out Hugo and Jeff paid Elizaveta and she got into a waiting taxi and rode away. He went over to them and said, "I saw you pay her." "So what," said Hugo, "didn't you know she was a whore."

VI The Autopsy

Shlomo went to the Abu Kabir Institute in Jerusalem for the results of the autopsy. This is where all autopsies are carried out in Israel. The pathologist was an older, white-haired man. He said "this was a terrible death, poor girl she must have suffered a lot before she died."

He explained to Shlomo, showing him X-rays and drawings, how the girl had died. She had been tied hand and foot, a small animal, a guinea pig, in a small sack had been inserted into her vagina. He said homosexuals use this way to get off, but in the anus, and it's rarer in females. However, there are pimps who do this to their girls and have men pay to witness it and they bet on when or if the animal can tear its way out of the sack. In the case of this girl it did, but apparently they weren't able to retrieve it in time. It bit her and she started to hemorrhage. Probably the guinea pig drowned in her blood. "Not a pleasant way to die!"

"About the young man, he was a bit older, about 25, he was beaten to death. He was punched many times and then kicked. You can clearly see the boot marks and the characteristic bruises."

Shlomo knew where he had to go next, he went to the Green Beach Hotel and asked if any of their guests were missing.
"Yes," came the reply, "a young man from Australia, hasn't been seen for about a week."
"Then take me to his room, has anything been disturbed, "
"Not by us." the clerk responded.

VII The Scotsman

Netanya is a seaside resort that was founded where there is a large ravine in the cliffs allowing access down over 100 feet (30 m) to the beach and the sea. Next to the sea on the cliff top is a large square, Kikar Ha'atzmaut (Independence Square) with a fountain and from there a pedestrian mall, called the Midrochov, leads inland. There are many restaurants in this area.

As Neil was passing one of them, the popular Scotsman, where the UN people on vacation usually ate, one of the waitresses, a Russian girl, ran out to him. "Are you Neil from Australia?" she asked. "Yes," he replied. "Wait a minute Elizaveta wants to see you."
With that, she ran back inside and immediately out came Elizaveta, running.

"Oh, Neil," she shouted, and ran up to him and grabbed him in her arms and kissed him passionately on the lips.

Neil was taken aback, he was not quite sure how to react, this was what he really wanted, but somehow he needed to act distant and annoyed. He disentangled himself from her and said, why did you invite me on the buggy-ride the other day with the other guys?"
"I wanted you, I would have done it with you for free, but I needed to earn their money."
He was confused by her answer, this was all too new, too much for him.

She pulled him towards her and kissed him again and whispered in his ear
"I love you, please save me!"
Save you from what, from whom? He wanted to ask, but he kept silent. Was it a desperate attempt to be taken away from her life, was he the chosen sucker, and what happened if they came after him.

She said, "Come back for me. I'm off in two hours."
"OK", he replied, but he made a mental note not to go back, not to get involved, not to save her.

But, he couldn't stand not knowing what was happening to her, so he called her number. A man answered and he spoke Russian-accented Hebrew. Neil asked to speak to Elizaveta. The man said "leave her alone, don't call here again, she isn't for you," and he hung up.

Neil didn't see Elizaveta at the Ulpan after that. He assumed whoever controlled her, her pimp, didn't want her mixing with other people, especially him. He tentatively asked about her to her friends, the other Russian girls. One of them took him aside and said, "her father sold her to the mob, best not to ask too many questions."

VIII The Diary

In going through Neil's things, Det. Shlomo Ben-Artzi discovered his diary. Actually, it was a collection of jottings, descriptions about the surroundings, comments about people and the beginnings of articles that he had thought of writing. In his comments the name Elizaveta stood out. She had apparently really made an impression on him. There was an attempt at a portrait of her and a photograph of a few girls at the Ulpan, and the face of one of them was circled. It was her, Shlomo recognized her as the dead girl.

At least now he had the identification of the two victims. He went back to the station and prepared a letter to be sent to the parents of the Australian boy. What a pity, he came to Israel to learn Hebrew and perhaps find a life for himself, and to end this way was too tragic. Something like this, a foreigner getting murdered was big news, both in Israel and Australia, and he knew he had to tread carefully.

The girl was less of a problem in a way. She was Russian and the Russian mob preyed on pretty young girls. They trafficked in illegal migrants, girls from Ukraine and Eastern Europe, many of whom were duped, expecting to start a good job, and they all ended up in brothels and walking the streets. But, if they were already here, it saved the mob the cost of importing them.

He went out and interviewed many of the people who had been at the Ulpan at the same time as Neil and Elizaveta. He focused on those in the same class. He interviewed Hugo and Jeff. He found the girls who were friends of Elizaveta and heard about her father.

He brought her father in for questioning under caution. He basically said it had nothing to do with him, he had to let her go to the mob, he had no choice.
"How much were you paid for her," Shlomo asked but could not get a specific reply. At least tell me who bought her from you. The father clammed up, but Shlomo got angry and physical, "I'll give you a name as long as you don't let them know it was me," he finally broke. The father named Vladimir Ruslansky, a well know local Jewish member of the Russian mob, who dealt in drugs, women, guns and anything else.

IX The Russian Mob

Shlomo knew where to find Ruslansky and his gang. He went to a small, ordinary side-street in the Old Industrial zone of Netanya, across the main highway from Tel Aviv to Haifa. He went into a coffee shop in a decrepit looking building. As he entered some of the gangsters stood up and went for their guns. Shlomo ignored them and swept past, thru the back door into an area of small offices and beyond that a large warehouse stacked with lots of cases and boxes.

He went into the first office and past the girl working there and into the inner office.
"Well, I am surprised to see you officer," said Vladimir Ruslanky, "what can I do for you," we have a nice choice of whisky if you like."
"You know why I'm here," Shlomo responded. "What happened with that girl and the Australian boy who were murdered on Green Beach."
"Oh, that little incident."
"Yes, that one."
"Well, first of all let me state that I had nothing to do with it. Second, I agree that it was regrettable that this poor boy had to get himself involved. But, the girl, she was just an unfortunate casualty of the need men have for unusual gratification. If it had only been her, she would have disappeared without a trace."
"Well, it was not only her, and the boy was involved."
"Well, what I hear is that this boy burst it and tried to release the girl, as a result the people in charge lost track of what was happening and things got out of hand. It

was an unfortunate accident. As you know Detective, accidents do happen."

"But, the boy's death was not an accident."

"No, Detective, but in his case, he attacked the men who were there and they defended themselves, it was a clear case of self-defense. Of course, I'm only telling you what I hear, I had no personal knowledge of this incident."

"So, in the end no one is responsible."

"Yes, unfortunately it seems that way. You could of course ask around, but I doubt that you'll find anyone who can tell you anything more."

Shlomo Ben-Artzi left the coffee shop with a hollow feeling in his stomach. How could he find those who had been present, how could be find out who actually beat the boy, and even if he did how could he get a charge to stick? He felt sick.

X The Entertainment

Neil arrived late at the Ulpan. As he went to sit down, one of the Russian girls came over to him. She said urgently, "Elizaveta said you should go to the Green Beach restaurant, she needs your help."

He replied, "I can't go now, I'll go after the lesson."

"No," she replied "It's urgent, very urgent, you must go now!" There was a tone in her voice that could not be ignored. He hesitated for a moment, and then left the class. He ran out into the parking lot and got into his car. He drove out of the Hotel back along the beach, sticking to the trail that led to the restaurant. Inside he saw a light, he parked the car and found the open door and rushed inside.

The scene that greeted him was chaotic, a large crowd of men milling around a brightly lit area.

He forced his way through the throng of men, some of them were screaming and shouting. In the center was a bright light and as he reached it he saw her, Elizaveta, spread-eagled naked on a large table, her hands and legs tied to it at the corners. She was covered in sweat and she was moving spasmodically, as if in ecstasy, in orgasm. He reached the table and looked down at her, she opened her eyes and smiled at him, she said something. He could not hear her over the shouting, he bent his head closer to hear her, she said "I knew you'd come," and then she closed her eyes again.

Even in that situation he saw again how beautiful she was. He started to try to release her from the grips of the table, but large hands grabbed him from behind and pulled him away, she became smaller as they dragged him away from her. He fought back, but it was in vain, they punched him and beat him, and although he fought back they pushed him to the ground and started to kick him. The last thing he saw was Elizaveta, her beautiful body writhing on the table in agony and ecstasy. Then the bright light went out.

Postscript: If you were to take the same road down through Poleg today (2013) you would find an entirely different perspective. There are now about 50 high rises that have been built in the past ten years. There are new roads and even a large Mall called Ir Yamim (City by the Sea). On the beach there are shops and the restaurant has been completely renovated. On the weekends crowds gather there to enjoy the beach, the sea and the sun. No-one remembers what happened there not so long ago.

The Perfect Spy

I Foreword

Growing up as a Jewish child in Germany in the late 1920s was hell. I was the oldest Jewish boy in our school and I was called names, "dirty Jew," tripped up, pushed around and beaten on a daily basis. The only way to protect me, since the teachers and the police wouldn't help, they laughed at my parents' complaints, was to send a car to take me and pick me up from school, but that only saved me from the worst of it.

When I was alone in my room I dreamed of being a strong, tough boy who could beat back these bullies and morons, but I knew that was impossible. Then I thought that maybe I could get a disguise so that they wouldn't recognize me, but I had distinctly Jewish features, a long nose and dark, curly hair. I wondered if it were possible to change my features, so that they wouldn't even think that I was Jewish.

I had become despondent, thinking of suicide, when I came across an article in a magazine about the new science of "cosmetic surgery." It was being developed in England. I did some more research and found out all the details. I showed it to my parents and then began a campaign of begging and cajoling them, until eventually when I was 15 in 1929 they relented and said they would pay for it. A nose job was known about, but I wanted more. So they sent me by train to London and from there to the hospital in the suburbs where they were performing face-changing surgery.

They asked me questions. I had learnt English at school and had studied in advance especially to answer these questions. Then after settling into a room, they came and marked my face. I asked them to reduce the size of my nose and also to remove my hair follicles so that I wouldn't be so dark. They also suggested to strengthen my weak chin and reduce my long forehead. I also asked them to make a permanent blond dye for my hair. They explained that it could not be permanent but would need updating every few weeks.

The surgery was painful, but I gritted my teeth and endured it. It made me stronger because I knew that I would no longer be a victim of that terrible abuse. After it was all done and I finally got to look at myself in the mirror I saw an incredible transformation, I looked Aryan, for me it was "too Aryan." How could I, a Jewish child have been so stupid as to think that changing my appearance could change my destiny. But, I was wrong, it did!

II The visit

One day, as I was healing, I was told that I had a visitor. I was very surprised and excited. I thought that perhaps my mother or other family member had come to see me. But, when the door opened it was an old man, or relatively old. He wore an old raincoat (you need that in England) and had rimmed glasses and grey hair. He came over and put out his hand to shake mine in a formal manner and said,

"How are you, are you healing well, you look splendid."

"I'm feeling much better, "I said, "but who are you?"

"That's a long story," he said in English, then switched to German "I'm an old friend of your parents."

"Strange they never told me about you."

'Yes, I understand why, when we left they disapproved. But now it seems that more Jews are trying to get out. Now that you are here, I thought you might like to convalesce at my place for a week or two after they release you from the hospital."

"But, I don't even know your name."

"Yes, of course, I'm Peter Schmidt, and I live not far from London. My wife and I would be delighted if you could accept our offer. You can write to your parents and let them know. I'll come and see you again, and I'll bring my car to pick you up afterwards. Here's my phone number in case you want to be in touch with me or to let me know when to pick you up."

He left and I thought, what a nice chap, but strange that Mum and Dad never mentioned him.

III Contact

While I was staying with Peter and his wife, Janet, in their nice house in the countryside, I began to relax and get used to my new looks. While I was there it turned into 1930. They introduced me to some boys and girls my own age and it was such a relief not to have to be on the defensive all the time, to be treated as a normal person. I enjoyed their company and I was introduced to drinking beer in the pub and various other English customs.

One of Peter's friends named Silas took an interest in me and invited me to visit his home for dinner. I was picked up and taken to his house. I had no idea where it was driving around in the dark. After we arrived Silas took me into a room and we sat down and he began to question me. I thought this is rather unusual, he's not just chatting with me, but in effect he's interrogating me. After a while answering questions about my childhood and the beatings and the names of those who mistreated me and my feelings about the Nazi party that was then an up and coming force, I suddenly stopped and asked him,

"Why are you interrogating me like this?"

"I wondered when you would react," he replied, without answering my question. So I repeated it.

"You see, we in Britain are very concerned. It doesn't take much imagination to see that the Nazi Party, if it ever got into power in Germany, could be a great threat to Britain and all that we stand for. As you know, in Germany anti-Semitism is endemic and rampant. Herr Hitler is using this culture to gain more power. He is already aiming to become Chancellor. We think that you are a friend of Britain, that you as a Jew and your family and friends will be greatly threatened by Hitler if he rises to power. We would like to help you. We would like to help bring your parents and your brothers and sisters to England. We will help them to settle in, and provide a house and schools and jobs for them. They will be looked after."

"Why would you do this? What do you want from me in return?"

"We only ask for your cooperation. You are now a new person, you look different than you did when you arrived in Britain. We have been following your progress and we see that you now can pass as an Aryan. We would like you to return to Germany under a different name and then report back to us what is happening in Germany, so that we can be well-informed by an independent observer. "

"Wait a minute, what you are asking is for me to become your spy," my heart was thumping furiously and my mouth went dry."

"In effect, yes."

"Wait, who are "we", how do I know I can trust you."

"We are the British secret services. I cannot tell you more at this stage. But, I can assure you this is a most serious proposition. We need eyes and ears in Germany.

You happened to fall into our lap, as it were. If you say "no" then you will go home to Germany and this conversation will be forgotten as if it never happened, but if you say "yes" we will train you to be able to protect yourself and to report back to us in secret. You would be able to strike a blow for those who will be persecuted under Hitler and the Nazis, and your family will be safe here, until there is a possibility for them to return to Germany when it is safe there."

I thought about it for a while in silence. Then I said, "when I came to Britain I wanted to change my appearance. Now I see that my change in appearance has made me into a potential asset for you. I am a Jew who can never accept the Nazi ideology. I now see that my change in appearance was only superficial, now I must adopt a new Aryan identity, so that I can fulfill my destiny. Yes, I agree."

"Good, then tonight you will return to Peter Schmidt's house and then tomorrow someone will pick you up. Don't worry about your parents. We have sent them letters in your name. They will be contacted and brought to Britain. But, it will be dangerous for you to meet them. You can speak to them by phone but not meet them. For their safety they must not know what you look like and what your new identity is. You have chosen a difficult and dangerous path, but we would not take you into our confidence if we did not think that you are capable of this difficult challenge."

IV Training

I was told that I would be transferred to Scotland for training. I envisaged this as very tough and I had to prepare myself mentally and physically for the outcome. I was put on a train to Edinburgh, where I was met at the station by a military man. He was an officer and he told me that from then on I was to act as if I were a soldier, a volunteer in Her Majesty's Forces, and that military justice would apply to me. I was taken to a remote castle that was also a barracks, and then to an office where I signed various papers.

I was attached to a group of young men from all over the world who were in training. Although we chatted and enjoyed each other's company, each of us guarded our identities and secrets very closely. Although I had a German accent that I could not hide, I carefully avoided speaking German.

We went out on forced marches carrying huge backpacks through barren countryside in the sleeting rain and did toughening up training, and learned close combat and judo. And parallel with this I was told my new identity, I was to be Wolfgang Schickel, a name that no Jewish German would have, and I was to be from a town nearby to my own, one that I knew well and had visited many times, Tubingen. But, not my own town in case anyone did recognize me. I had to come from a non-Jewish neighborhood in that town, and I was rehearsed in the street names and bus routes and football teams and schools, over and over again until I knew that town like the back of my hand (as the English said).

But, it was not all hard work and training. We had a well-stocked bar in the castle, and we were allowed to drink and enjoy ourselves on weekends. There were even some young women in training there, and we had great fun together. They had an insignia on their uniforms that was "FYC." I think it stood for "Female Youth Corps," but they said it was "Fuck for your country" and I must say they were very skilled at it. I suspect that they were a bunch of young prostitutes who had been brought in for training also to do spying work, and they were allowed to practice on us. It was a great experience for me, since I had no previous experience of sex. Maybe that was part of my training too.

But, before I could be released on the world I had one thing that had to be taken care of. I was circumcised, and I could not pass as an Aryan without having this taken care of. So I submitted myself to another operation that with local anesthetic proved not to be so painful to reverse this procedure.

I lost track of time there and after learning parachuting and gaining weight and being taught how to defend myself and shoot guns, I felt that I was ready for the big time.

V Captured

I was told to go by train to London for a meeting. With my new Aryan identity I was quite happy to step out into the real world again. I was given instructions where to go. I was to take a cab from the station in London near to the destination and then walk the rest of the way.

At the station I entered a taxi and gave the driver an address. He drove for a while and then he suddenly stopped. Two men got into the cab on either side of me. I was instantly alarmed, but before I could react a needle was pushed into my arm thru my sleeve and I quickly began to lose consciousness

When I awoke I was trussed up inside a case. I could tell it was a wooden packing case. I was afraid. I thought for a minute that this might be a kind of test, but would they treat me quite so badly. The case was moved around and I was bumped as it was lifted and then dropped into place. Then I felt the rocking of a train and I realized I was being transported. I tried to cry out but my mouth was covered. I could not release my hands or arms or feet. I lost consciousness again. Later when I woke up I felt I was in a ship. I could feel the rocking and the waves breaking against the hull. Where were they taking me?

Time seemed to pass incredibly slowly. I was cold, thirsty and hungry. I seemed I have been in this case for days. Yet, I knew that they were transporting me for a reason, they wouldn't let me die in there. Finally I felt the ship dock and the case was lifted into a lorry, and was driven to an unknown destination.

I awoke to hear the box being broken open and the sound of German voices. I shuddered, now I knew where I was, I was back in Germany. I had been snatched from London and brought back to Germany. But, how could they have known. They must have been watching me, or someone in the British services had given me away, a traitor. If I lived to escape this terrible predicament I would find and kill that bastard.

When the box was opened I found myself in a dark cellar with three men around me. They extracted me from the box and sat me on a chair. They shouted oaths at me in German. They called me the usual slanders that I had grown up with, "dirty Jew" "pig bastard," and so on. It angered me to be called these names, now that I looked Aryan and had a new Aryan identity. I begged for a drink, and they gave me water, and then something to eat. They released my hands so I could eat, but they had tied me to the chair so I could not move

After a while someone else came into the room. He sat opposite me at the table and began to talk to me. He said "we know who you are Herr Schickel, we have been following you and we know you are a plant from the

British secret service. We will spare your life if you cooperate with us." I immediately realized that they were using my name from my new German passport that I was carrying. They suspected me, yet they did not know my true identity.

I was interrogated many times by different men with different approaches. Some were vicious and struck me, others were friendly and tried to coax information out of me. They asked me about my childhood, my parents, my background, my friends. I had all these answers, but it was difficult not to get mixed up and reveal something about my true identity. On a few occasions I slipped up, but luckily they seemed not to notice. Overall they fed me well and I was able to become friendly with a few of the guards, who I thought were soldiers. But it was difficult to ascertain where we were, from the occasional sounds of ships horns and the time I had been in the ship I guessed that we were either in Kiel or Hamburg.

I was allowed to walk around freely in my basement cell and gradually days and nights became blurred. Yet I never lost sight of the fact that I must convince these captors that I was really who I said I was and then get out so that I could fulfill my destiny.

Then one day I heard shouting and gunfire and realized that there was a gunfight going on outside my cell. The door was blown open and some soldiers with guns ran in and shot the guards. I was grabbed by these men and hustled out, and through a maze of tunnels and out through a door into a waiting car. Then once again I felt a needle in my arm and blacked out.

When I regained consciousness this time I was back in the Castle in Scotland with a group of my trainers and teachers around me.

"What happened?" I asked in astonishment. "We rescued you," they said and laughed and joked about it. "Where was I?" I asked plaintively," "Oh you were in the basement of this castle," they said and laughed uproariously. "What," I said, "It was all a set-up?" "Don't worry, you passed with flying colors, you withstood the interrogation and you gave nothing away." "How did you trick me?" "Oh, it was easy, we simply put you on a boat back to Scotland and then brought you to the castle and our men interrogated you."

"I don't believe it!"

"Yes, it was very convincing, would you like to meet your interrogators?" and he ushered in a few of the men who had in fact been my interrogators, who now were smiling and wearing British uniforms. They said, "Have a drink, Herr Schickel."

"But, the ship sirens?" "Oh, a simple recording."

"But, the guards, they were shot." "No it was red paint, very convincing."

"How long was I there?"

"Only a few days, we tricked you by gradually shortening the lengths of days and nights. I hope you learned something from this little experience, first always be on your guard and second don't believe everything you see or hear."

VI Into the Maelstrom

I took the train across the channel to Paris and after a few days moved on to Berlin. It was now 1931 and things were heating up in Germany. Hitler had managed to overcome his electoral deficiency and had received over 18% of the popular vote in the last election. But, there was political stalemate, and violence on the streets. I joined a group of Nazis in a kind of barracks in the east of the city near Potsdam, and every day we went out on skirmishes, breaking up Jewish businesses and attacking communist headquarters. I wore a black shirt and joined the party. I tried to focus my attention on the anti-communist actions rather than the anti-Jewish ones, but I had to be careful not to draw too much attention to myself.

Nevertheless my fervor was noticed and I was put in charge of a cadre of anti-communist militants. We found the list of communist members and went to their homes and attacked them. Meanwhile two more elections took place in 1932, and from the chaos Hitler emerged with over a third of the votes. Finally, after the vote in 1933 when the Nazis received 44%, Hindenberg stood aside and supported Hitler for Chancellor. We celebrated wildly when Hitler was declared Chancellor on January 30, 1933. From then on we were in charge!

Our orders now changed. We were to infiltrate the police and the army. I volunteered for the new armed police force that was under the command of Heinrich Himmler, known as the SS and was put in the operational command office in Berlin. I was required to take the oath of allegiance unto death to the Fuhrer Adolf Hitler and I received a code number that was tattooed under my left armpit. I received military training and volunteered as a radio transmitter. This was a planned move since it meant I could then start to transmit to my own contacts back in England (carrying a radio around would have been too conspicuous).

When I had privacy, I first sent out my contact code very briefly on the special wavelength and at the prearranged time. Then later I sent another message in code, simply stating "SS officer." They would understand. At that time there was no effective monitoring of radio transmissions going out of Berlin. It was not until later that the SS introduced stringent control of all radio transmitters and started to triangulate to find the source of unauthorized transmissions. I had no way of knowing if my messages were received, but I expected they were listening intently for any sign of life.

After the Reichstag Fire in February 1933, the Weimar Republic was officially ended and Hitler took power as the Reichschancellor. Then I was transferred to the armed SS regiment that was preparing for war. As a radio officer I had access to the transmitters most of the time and conveyed the changing situation to London.

VII The Eastern Front

In Germany people were very excited when Hitler annexed the Sudetenland in 1939 and then attacked Poland and divided it between Germany and the Soviet Union according to the German-Russian non-aggression pact. After this, in September 1939, Britain declared war on Germany. It was then that my reports back to Britain became more important. I kept my eyes and ears open, I asked around, I started sending longer coded reports. I knew that this was dangerous, but this was my job. I sent them troop estimates, troop movements, train routes used, names of officers, etc, etc.

However, operating in Berlin became more and more dangerous as the SS became more vigilant. As a member of the SS, I was not under suspicion, but I had to be very careful. In 1940 I began to hear reports of huge troop movements towards Russia and I passed these on to the British. In 1941 this resulted in Operation Barbarossa (red-beard) when German troops attacked the Soviet Union over a huge front. Although I had warned the British, the Soviets under Stalin were apparently either not warned or did not believe the warnings, because they were unprepared for this onslaught, and at first the progress was rapid. Now most of Europe, from the coast of France to the steppes of Russia, was under Nazi domination, and my comrades were ecstatic about it. I transmitted to Britain that the German people were fully supportive of Hitler's conquests.

Now the place to be was the Eastern Front, and my unit volunteered to be sent there. At that time it was not the death sentence that it later became. We were sent with the head-quarter's unit of the Waffen SS that had become a separate Nazi Army, affiliated with the Wermacht, but separate from it and still under Nazi party orders.

The further east we went the more desperate the conditions became. Now we saw for ourselves the massacres that we had heard rumors about, mainly of Jews. We would arrive at a village, the Jews would be separated out and over the course of a day or two they were massacred, often with the active participation of the local population. I could do nothing to stop this. I duly reported the actions to London. It was actually safer to transmit from out there than from Berlin.

When we were stationed in a location for some time I noticed that Jewesses were brought into a house near the HQ, and this was used as a brothel for the officers and men. Now under the Nuremberg Laws of racial purity of 1935, racial mixing was forbidden. Miscegenation, especially of Germans with Jews was strictly forbidden. I saw an opportunity to help the Jewish women, so I complained to my superiors about this, and they laughed at me. They said, "why not enjoy the sluts, we are going to kill them anyway." They thought I was a Nazi purist.

So I wrote a letter to SS HQ in Berlin complaining about these common practices. I pointed out that Jews were being removed from German society for the express purpose of preventing miscegenation, and German citizens could be arrested and charged for this criminal offense under the German law. Yet here on the Eastern Front, such miscegenation was occurring with deliberate official inaction, they were looking the other way. I said this should not be accepted, and furthermore the sex and killings by the German Army itself was demoralizing the soldiers. I knew that I was not supposed to draw attention to myself, but I had to do something, and I was not alone in feeling this way. There were murmurings among some of the officers that things were getting out of hand and that women were being raped indiscriminately.

It took some months for me to get a reply. I was told that the Control Section of the Waffen SS was disturbed by the situation I reported and would issue strict orders that Jewesses should not be used in any way for sexual activity. Soon after, orders were issued through the chain of command to stop these practices. On several occasions I discovered soldiers in the process of raping women, Jews and non-Jews, and I stopped them. I usually took the women in my car and dropped them near a train station and gave them some money and told them to get on the next train and get away from there, as far as possible. I never revealed my name or any Jewish affiliation in case they were captured and tortured.

Perhaps because of my action, I was called back to Berlin for re-assignment in June, 1941. I was interviewed in the office of Reichsmarshall Goering and then told that I had been selected to be the officer in charge of the radio transmissions from the Fuhrer's new eastern headquarters called *Wolfsschanze* or "The Wolf's Lair" situated near Rastenburg in Poland. This was a very honored position, and I was happy to transmit the information to London that I had been selected for this position. It also meant that London and the allies knew immediately of the secret location of the *Wolfsschanze*, that could be used for future bombing, etc. However, the security there was very tight, the location was surrounded by three layers of security, and was virtually impenetrable. But, the Britsh secret service had a valuable agent inside the Lair, me.

As time went by the Fuhrer spent more and more time living at the *Wolfsschanz*. He took personal charge of the action on the Eastern Front, to the distress of his Generals. According to the comments I overheard, Hitler made two errors that proved very costly for the German Army. Before Moscow and Stalingrad he divided his forces. He hoped to bring a large pincers movement to bear on Moscow, but each of the pincers proved too weak to succeed against the Russian forces. And he underestimated the resistance at Stalingrad and sent half his forces on a wild goose chase into the Caucasus to try to capture the oil fields of Persia and Azerbaijan (Baku), which they never succeeded in reaching. I duly reported these developments to my handlers in Britain, who must have been amazed at the detailed and significant information I was able to provide.

Not only did I rely for intelligence on the radio transmissions I legitimately sent to Berlin and to the commanders in the field as part of my job, but I also heard the comments and gossip that was going around. Having a girl-friend, Hansel Kraut, who worked as a secretary in the office of the commanding officer of Hitler's staff was also very helpful.

VIII The Attempt

After about a year at the *Wolfsschanze,* the security suddenly put on a search that everyone was required to undergo. They asked me the usual questions, but I had rehearsed this a million times and I knew all the answers, about why I was in Berlin "that was where the action was," and why I joined the SS, "because I truly believe in the Fuhrer's programs, "and so on.

But, then they asked me why I had hydrogen peroxide and blonde hair dye in my personal possessions. For a moment I was flumoxed, but then I thought of an answer. I told them that I was seeing Hansel Kraut, the secretary in the typing pool and she needed a top up every now and then for her blond hair. They accepted that, but I had no idea if they actually asked Hansel about this.

It was through my contact with Hansel that I first heard about the planned attempt on Hitler's life. In July, 1944, the word was going around that there was a group of officers who were fed up with Hitler's conduct of the war. It was understood that these were German patriots, who saw the destruction that was being wrought on Germany by the Allies and were sure that Germany would lose the war. To even whisper this was considered traitorous and could get you killed. But, lovers could whisper this to each other in the intimacy of an embrace. Hansel asked me if I wanted to be put in contact with one of the conspirators, and I balked. I told her I sympathised with their aims, but I could not join them. I let her think that I was still a true devotee of the Fuhrer.

I passed this information onto London. So I was not surprised when the bomb went off in the morning of July 20, 1944. At first many of us were shocked, but could not reveal our happiness until we were sure that Hitler was dead. In fact, I was the one who had to send the message to Berlin that the Fuhrer was still alive, and later that day he gave a live radio broadcast to the nation. In fact I had sent the details of the explosion and the unfortunate outcome to London even before the plotters landed in Berlin. The names of the plotters soon became known and several of them were shot that evening. I passed on the nature of the plot and the names of the plotters to London. They knew that unfortunately Hitler would remain in charge of Germany for the foreseeable future.

IX The Russians

As winter enveloped the Wolf's Lair in October, 1944, it was rumored that the Red Army was no more than a few days away. Nevertheless Hitler stayed until November 20, and then left with little celebration. Several days later orders arrrived to destroy the whole complex. It was my job to destroy the communications equipment. Nevertheless I kept a small transmitter hidden under the rubble of the transmission hut. Huge explosions ripped through the edifice, but they were not enough to obliterate the enormous concrete emplacements that were supposed to last for 1,000 years.

Orders were given for various units to return to Germany, but I realized that Hitler's time was numbered and for me to go back into that hated country would be suicidal. I decied to try my luck with the Russians. I was after all a British agent, an ally of theirs. So I made my last transmission, destroyed the equipment and ditched my uniform, then made my way towards the Russian lines. I was not alone, a few German stragglers did the same.

Now I was thankful for the training I had received that seemed ages ago in Scotland, trudging through a sleeting rain with zero visibility. I had a compass and not much else to guide me. I simply went east, hoping soon to come across some Russian soldiers. But, it was not as simple as that, there was after all a front line and to cross it I had to avoid German soldiers in retreat and avoid being shot by Russian soldiers who were indiscriminantly shooting Germans. I decided not to speak German to them, I knew some Russian and also some Yiddish, and I hoped that would get me through. Also there was the little matter of the SS number tatooed under my arm and the fact that I was well-fed and certainly not a Jewish survivor. Anyway, who would believe that I was Jewish or even a British agent in that place and time.

When I heard shooting I headed straight in that direction. I could not spend a night out in those conditions, even with my training. As I was floundering around two figures appeared miraculously before me in the white mist, they were all dressed in white, and appeared like angels, but in their hands they carried sub-machine guns. I knew immediately that they were Russians because the German Army had not issued winter gear to their soldiers, another of Hitler's terrible mistakes.

I immediately put up my hands in surrender and shouted in Russian that I was a friend. They aimed their guns at me, but began talking in Russian, and I could not understand them, so I kept repeating what I had said and then I said some words in English. I told them I was a British soldier from London and wanted to see their superior officer. I repeated the word "officer" several times in Russian. They were really confused by this, and finally after checking that I had no guns they dragged me away and turned me over to some other soldiers, who marched me down a road into a camp. There I was taken into a hut and handcuffed, although they gave me some water and soup to drink.

An officer came in and started talking to me in German. I replied in German and English, he did not understand my English but he recognized what it was, and so he went out and brought in an officer who spoke a few words of English. He explained to the other officer what I told him, that I was a British spy who had been working under cover with the Germans, and I could prove it. I asked them to bring the radio operator and I told him a frequency to transmit on. I told him if he gave them some information about me being captured by the Russians, he would have a reply on another frequency that he could specify that would confirm my story. Sure enough about an hour after the transmission he received a reply in Russian in the clear saying that I was a British officer and giving my id number, that I had given them.

But, of course, they were not convinced, fearing a trick, so they turned me over to the KGB. The men in leather coats came and picked me up in a car and drove me for some hours to a lock-up. They took off my clothes and examined me in great detail. They of course found the number tatooed under my arm and knew that I was SS. But, since I claimed to be a British officer and spoke English they were very confused. When I realized that one of the Russians was Jewish I threw in a few words of Yiddish, and that really confused them.

Finally, I was taken before a senior KGB Colonel, who interrogated me in a mixture of German and English. I told him all he had to do was contact the British authorities and they would vouch for the fact that I was a British officer. I told him about my plastic surgery, about my training in Britain, and my job as the wireless operator at Hitler's eastern headquarters, where I had transmitted important secret information to the British that had undoubtedly been passed on to the Soviet authorites and had hopefully saved many Russian soldier's lives. He listened patiently and then said "you are SS and I don't believe you."

I was transferred to another location but kept in a cell. Then I was flown for several hours to another city. I was again interrogated, but kept to my story, which although it was complex and confusing was in fact the truth. Then I was flown to Moscow and once again interrogated by a more senior KGB General. They kept me in prison, although I was not mistreated, and gradually my hair began to grow in its normal black colour. When I pointed this out to the interrogators they found it very amusing, but it did fit in with my story. Over a period of months they debriefed me, about my experiences in Britain, in the SS and in the Wolfsschanze.

Finally they allowed a visit with a British representative and after this they released me into his custody. I learnt that the war was coming to an end. I flew over Germny on the way to Britain and I saw that it was largely destroyed and in ruins. I felt sorry for Germany. Once I had been a proud German, but their treatment of me had relieved me of that sentiment. I was glad that I had played a role in defeating the criminal Nazi regime.

When I returned to Britain I was once again de-briefed in detail over a period of months, but I was able to go around, visit with my parents and enjoy some good food and drink. What a wonderful feeling to have survived what I had been through.

X Epilogue

After a few years living somewhat aimlessly in Britain, I heard about the imminent war in the Middle East and offered my services to the main Jewish military organization, the Haganah. I went secretly to Palestine, where my British passport was valid and my training and experience in military matters was invaluable.

Many Jews had volunteered for the British forces to fight Nazism, and now after the Holocaust they returned to Palestine in order to fulfil their destiny to establish a Jewish State. I helped to develop a new wireless corps for the emerging Jewish force. When the Israeli State was declared by David Ben Gurion in 1948, I helped to establish its military intelligence service.

Now, many years later, I look around at my children and grandchildren and am glad to say that none of them needs plastic surgery in order to live happy and fulfilling lives in our own Jewish State.

Jutland

I

It's quite possible that I became an actor to resolve certain, shall we say, contradictions, in my life. Being in the role of another person meant for me an escape from the drab reality of everyday life, but also from the past that haunted me. But, what actually was that past? It was never clear to me. It drifted in and out of my consciousness. What could be so terrible that even my mind could not allow me to know it. People became schizophrenic for less.

When I was a child my skill at mimicking others was noticed and I was put in school plays and given leading roles. My parents were very supportive of this, they were probably glad that their troubled and disruptive child had found something to be good at, something to distract him from his otherwise difficult childhood. I noticed that when I was acting I tended to be less troublesome and, in my secret personal world, less self-harming. The need to dig scissors into myself and cut myself was lessened.

When I was a young teenager I took to drugs, it seemed natural to me, and sometimes in a drug-induced haze I would cut my legs or arms with a razor or even burn myself. I had no idea why I did this, to me it was normal.

One day when my mother noticed that I was bleeding she dragged me to the hospital and they discovered my secret and sent me to a psychiatrist. That's where I learnt words like schizophrenic and self-harming.

My chats with the psychiatrist became a regular part of my life, and I suppose they did help me, although I could never reveal the angst that was lurking deep inside me. It was during this time that I remembered some terrible things, that I could not articulate, and I realized also that I was probably adopted. Often I would have an image of a woman hanging and of being hurt by knives or being burnt, and I would wake up screaming at night. I also remembered people speaking in a strange tongue that I could not decipher and of being tormented by other children.

In our graduating year my school decided to put on Shakespeare's "Hamlet," and although I was never a scholarly child, I somehow took to it. Even though I could not understand everything in the play, I felt sympathy for the troubled lad, we shared certain things in common. My acting was noted in the local newspaper and people came to see me in the play. Soon I was in acting school and given roles in dramas and my acting skills were noticed. I auditioned for a part in a movie and got the part. My blond good looks evidently helped me. I left New York and moved out to Hollywood, and there I became a star.

It all seemed like a dream to me, life as a facsimile of reality. Of course, I entered into the boozy, druggy life there with great enthusiasm. Some days I would wake up by the pool with a hangover with a young girl sleeping with me, and not even know who I was or where I was.

During one of my visits back home, my mother had taken me aside and told me that at least I should know, now that I was grown up, that I had been adopted. That my birth mother had died and I was an orphan and they had wanted a child and so they had adopted me. I knew that I had not been their natural child, they were so calm and I was so troubled, there was a disconnect. I thanked her and asked her who had been my mother, but she told me that she didn't know and that it would be better if I didn't know either.

During one of my sober periods, I decided to research this mysterious woman who had been my biological mother. I managed to contact the psychiatrist who had treated me early on, and he confirmed that I had been adopted. By going to court, using the excuse of medical necessity, I managed to obtain the name of the agency that had arranged my adoption and eventually found the identity of my mother. Her name had been Ophelia Ericson. It was with great surprise and concern that I discovered that she had been of Danish origin, and that she had been arrested several times for prostitution. Her death certificate showed that at the age of 20 she had hung herself.

She came from a village in the center of the Jutland district of Denmark and had moved to New York in 1951 when she was 18 and when I was only 5 years old. I began to remember snippets of this voyage by ship and of living with my mother in Greenwich Village. I even found the address, a seedy, poor location. Now that I was a famous film actor, I could afford to indulge my intense curiosity. I decided to visit Denmark to see for myself where she had come from and why she had left at such an early age to live alone in a foreign country far away.

I wrote to her parents and they were very surprised and delighted to hear from me after so many years. They said they had lost contact with their daughter and had only found out after the event that I had been adopted. Because of the secrecy involved they could not find out who my adoptive parents were and so had never expected to hear from me again. So I, their natural grandson, flew to Denmark in 1976 with great anticipation to discover my mother's story.

II

The older Ericsons, my grandparents, were indeed lovely people. They gave me their spare bedroom to sleep in, that had been my mother's room many years before. After we had got to know each other I broached the difficult question to them, why had my mother gone alone to New York at the age of 18, with me a young child? They spoke English well, but they found it difficult if not impossible to explain to me what had happened. All they would say was that it had been a different world then, and they would quickly change the subject.

At the local bar I was approached by a few men of my age, who introduced themselves. They remembered me, and knew that my mother had left for New York, but were not very communicative. After the others left, one guy continued to talk to me, perhaps his tongue loosened by the alcohol, and he admitted that they had mistreated me at school, but he would not explain why.

Sleeping in my mother's bedroom was both comforting and disturbing for me. I found solace in the fact that I had found my roots, but I had to face up to the fact that she had abused me and become a prostitute and had then committed suicide. Something in her background had so affected her that she had left home at the earliest opportunity to go to a foreign land and had then been disturbed and self-destructive.

After I had been staying with them for a few days, the Ericsons asked me to sit with them and then told me that they had some papers that she had left and some letters that my mother had sent them after she had arrived in New York. They gave them to me, a sheaf of old papers, written in Danish. They asked me to keep them and to read them when I could have them translated, and then perhaps they would help me to understand.

I took them to a translator in Copenhagen and she explained to me that some parts of the papers were a kind of journal that my mother had kept when she was a girl, from the age of 13 or so until she left Denmark, and the others were letters she had sent from New York, that seemed more intended as a continuation of the diary than normal letters.

III

I remember that I was playing in our garden, it was in late 1945 when I was 12, and it suddenly seemed very quiet. I looked up and through the gate I saw some men walking by. I was curious so I went to see what was going on. I immediately recognized them as German soldiers.

They were walking slowly and carrying their guns by their sides and their uniforms were disheveled. They were not anything like the German soldiers I remembered from a few years before when they had passed by our village, and my father had taken me to see them. Then they had marched in tight formation, guns sloped on their shoulders and very smart and gleaming. Then they had been marching north, now they were walking south, back towards Germany.

I called out to them "what's the matter with you?" One young soldier looked at me with surprise and came towards me. He said "fraulein, why don't you come with us to glorious Germany." I remember the tone in his voice, monotonous and frightening. I turned to run back towards the house, but he quickly reached out and grabbed my hair and pulled me around the gate into the lane. I screamed and my mother came running out towards me. The soldier and several others leveled their guns at her, and she backed away screaming "don't take my daughter, don't take my daughter!"

They marched me with them for a few miles, until they found a barn where they put their things down inside and settled down to cook a meal and rest. My soldier took me into the back of the barn where there was hay stored and he pulled off my clothes and pushed me onto the ground and then he raped me. I screamed a lot, but he hit me and told me to be quiet. After he was done, other men came and raped me. I heard them arguing, whether or not they should do this and who would be next. This went on for what seemed like an eternity. Believe me when I say that I had no choice.

After they had finished with their eating and drinking and with me, they began to pack up to leave. One of the soldiers came toward me with his bayonet fixed and stuck it into me. I felt a severe pain and passed out. I awoke to the smell of burning. Evidently he had not killed me, whether by accident or design. I realized that they had set fire to the barn on leaving. Suddenly I heard my name being called, and my mother came through the smoke towards me. I wanted to stay there and be cleansed by the fire, but she dragged me out. I dimly remember being lifted up into the air and then floating back towards my bed.

The resistance had been told about the platoon of German soldiers and had set up an ambush for them. They were caught unprepared and most of them were killed. Those that were not dead were tortured and mutilated. I was taken to see this scene of carnage, as if it might help heal my suffering. But, seeing the corpses with their genitals severed did not help my mental state.

Then I discovered that I was pregnant. I had the baby when I was 13. I was different from all the other children, I had a baby and it was a German bastard. I lived with this misfortune for five years, putting up with the whispering, the innuendos and the hostility. At school my son was treated like a leper, no children would play with him, they ostracized him and beat him and he was in a terrible state. Added to which I could hardly call myself a proper mother. I half hated him for bringing this situation upon me, for reminding me every day of the terrible circumstances under which he had been conceived. At the earliest opportunity, when I reached 18, I left home and took him to New York, away from that terrible place.

But, there I found it very difficult to manage, to get a job and to integrate. One day coming home from work I was accosted by a black man. He seemed to know about me, he knew my name and he offered to get me a good job. He was friendly and I soon took up his offer, only to find myself working in a brothel. Perhaps my experience in life had prepared me for this miserable existence, serving men for their pleasure.

My son was often neglected, but I managed to feed and clothe him, but I could not be a proper mother to him. I blamed him for my predicament. And so I decided that there was no escape for me, and I decided to do away with myself, to leave this miserable existence. I figured that my son could not be worse off without me, and perhaps he would find loving parents, who could give him a life like I never could.

Meningioma

I was talking to Andy at the reception after my inaugural lecture to the Department that I had recently joined. Towards the end of the lecture I had the recurrence of a terrible stabbing headache in the left frontal region. I was still quite excited, I felt I had given a good lecture and Andy was congratulating me, when he suddenly disappeared!

I continued to talk to him, but I was really shocked, I shook my head. Suddenly he reappeared. What was happening? I was not sure, was it real? Then momentarily it happened again. I said to him "you just disappeared as I was speaking to you and you just came back." Since he knew me and he was a physician he reacted in a sober way, he asked me "where exactly did I disappear?"
"From the left hand side of my vision, it was as if there was a strip that I could not see."
"I think you should go and see a doctor as soon as possible. There could be several causes for something like that. I think it may be because you are excited by the lecture, that may have triggered it."

The next day I went to see my GP, an older man whom I greatly respected. He tested my eyes, and said he could find nothing wrong and then said that I should go to see a brain surgeon! I was shocked. He said that such incidents were often an indication of something wrong in the optic nerve or the brain. He looked in his reference book and found a specialist locally who had a great deal of experience in this area.

The following week I went to see the specialist at the George Washington Hospital Center. He was the Head of the Department of Neurosurgery and he was highly recommended. He had practiced previously at the Mayo Clinic, so he must be good. After hearing my story and examining me, I said to him that I could not understand why I was seeing a brain surgeon after one such incident. He said I was lucky, usually these incidents are warnings of something amiss, and I should heed the warning and take his advice. He sent me to have an MRI the following day.

My wife accompanied me in the middle of the night, because it was cheaper then. We went down in the elevator underground to where the MRI machine was located. Since I had some expertise in the MRI area I knew about the machine and its technology, although I suppose for someone not knowledgeable it might have been a rather frightening experience to be slid into the middle of the huge metal cylinder and then when the machine was working it sounded like a machine gun going off in your head. But, I knew that was the sound of the pulsed magnetic field gradients switching.

Three days later I went to see the surgeon with the results. He informed me that from the analysis of the radiologist and from his own experience it was clear that I had a small growth on my optic nerve between the optic chiasma, where the two optic nerves crossed, and the brain. He showed it to me, a faint areola glowing in the dark recesses of my head that normally should not be there. It was highly likely, about 90%, he said that the growth was benign, and it was very likely that it was a meningioma. The meninges, he went on to explain, is the envelope that encloses the brain, and it is quite common for small benign growths to develop on it. These usually grow very slowly and give no symptoms and are often found only after death. But, rarely, they grow in places where they cause problems, such as on the optic nerve. He had operated on about 40 such cases. Before he made a definitive decision he wanted me to have another MRI with contrast agent.

The contrast agent, as in X-rays, highlights certain regions and provides a more definitive picture. I was injected with the agent prior to having another series of MR images. In my case it worked brilliantly, the slight glow lighted up like a bright star. Later the surgeon explained that it was because the growth had its own blood vessels and the contrast agent goes through them and lights it up, whereas the rest of the surrounding space in the inferior fossa shows no increased intensity. He explained that this result was highly diagnostic of a meningioma since it usually had a good blood supply compared to most other possible growths (I felt on several occasions that he was on the point of calling it a tumor, but he avoided that). He advised me that I should have it removed surgically. This was elective surgery, in that it was not imminently dangerous. But, if not removed it could permanently damage my sight.

I asked if he minded if I got a second opinion and he said of course not, I should get one, since it was major surgery and I should be certain before I made a decision. So I went to another brain surgeon (probably a friend of his). But, the story was the same. He told me of the case of a young woman some 10 years before who had exactly the same symptoms as me, but then they did not have MRI to definitively show the presence of the growth, and she did not have surgery. After about two years she began to go blind and there was nothing they could do about it. So I was "lucky" that it had been caught early in my case and they knew exactly where it was.

He explained that because the growth was on the right optic nerve before the chiasma that the symptoms would be felt on the left side. He told me that the growth of the meningioma would cause it to press on the optic nerve causing blindness. Also during periods of high blood pressure (such as giving a lecture!) it would swell, hence producing the symptoms I had experienced. If it should burst then it would irretrievably damage the optic nerve and I would become blind, hence he recommended that I should have it removed as soon as possible.

On a model of the cranium he showed me how they would have to enter the skull by removing a small piece (that they would put back afterwards). I remember distinctly that he said the brain would then "flop to one side" and then they would be able to get underneath it to remove the growth on the optic nerve. I sat there in what seemed a normal world contemplating having my skull opened up and having what amounted to "brain surgery." He emphasized that it was not brain surgery, they would not touch my brain, but that it would have to be done intra-cranially. However, he stated that such operations, although major surgery, were essentially routine, and my surgeon was one of the best in the world for that particular operation.

So it was that barely three weeks after suffering a single incident of partial blindness I found myself entering the Hospital to have intra-cranial surgery on a meningioma on my right optic nerve. I knew that I had to do this, but I was scared.

I remember nothing about the operation itself. From the time I was given the first injection to the time a few days later that I became fully conscious no memory remains. Apparently the operation took 4 hours and went very well. The removal of the meningioma was done by micro-surgery. I was told a few days later that during the process it was found that the growth had extended to the base of the pituitary gland and that in removing it the tiny stalk of the gland had been damaged. This had been mentioned previously as a possible side effect of the surgery, since the pituitary was very close and the stalk very fine. Apart from this the operation had been fully successful. But, it would mean that I would have to take some steroid hormones for the rest of my life.

My wife was wonderful. She sat and held my hand and showed her evident relief that I was alive and vital after the traumatic experience. There was a wonderful black assistant doctor who helped me a lot, and altogether it looked as if I would recover completely. One day my daughter was visiting me and we decided to call my wife, as I was on the phone, and once again I have no recollection of this at all, I suddenly stopped talking and dropped the phone. My daughter immediately called the nurse who called the doctor, and she also spoke to my wife and told her to come immediately.

I don't know what they did, but I came around and within a short while I was back to normal. Apparently these seizures are quite common after cranial surgery. But, it was a shocking experience for us. Luckily I had an endocrinologist who came to see me, he looked at what they were giving me in the constant drip, and realized that it was deficient in potassium. The nerve system requires potassium and somehow after such an operation it requires more than usual. So he told them, and after they upped the potassium I never had a recurrence. I also started eating bananas that are rich in potassium.

Once I was able to get up I went to look at myself in the bathroom mirror. Of course it was difficult to see anything because of the copious bandages. I looked like a mummy. But, when they took the bandages off I saw that I had a vicious red scar from the hair line above my right eye to above the ear. Of course, this would have been covered by hair if I had any. The little I had left had been completely shaved off. My right face was all bruised and my right eye was blood red. I looked hideous, I hardly recognized myself. Perhaps I was someone else, a discontinuity, or like one of those movies where the villain has plastic surgery and changes his identity.

In a few days I was home, gradually shuffling around relearning how to do simple things. Since I found it tiresome to speak I took to pointing and grunting. I usually got what I wanted. Gradually I recovered and in two weeks I was almost back to normal. My job was safe and they were incredibly helpful, especially given that I was new there. They said take a vacation, and since there was a meeting in Florida only two weeks later that I had previously signed up for, I decided to go. So four weeks after the operation, with my face returning to normal and my hair growing, I was in Clearwater and gave my lecture. It was a short one and I was quite careful, sitting on the beach, walking around, nothing too strenuous.

My colleagues were generally very nice about it, and I joked around with them about the surgeon having found no brain, etc. But I discovered later that this was a mistake, because everyone thought that I had had brain surgery, and the word got around, spread by certain malicious rivals, that indeed my mental processes had been impaired, whereas actually my brain had not been touched and I was quite normal in that respect.

However, I was taking many pills, including high levels of steroid. This was gradually reduced, but I was told that given the damage to my pituitary gland, I would have to take a low maintenance level every day for the rest of my life. Not a bad outcome. Also, since all my hormonal system was affected, as the pituitary is a master gland that stimulates many others, I would have to take a thyroid replacement, and I would have to have shots of testosterone. Suddenly it hit me I would be functionally impotent unless I kept taking the male hormone. I had never envisaged this as an outcome of the surgery. Still, it was a lot better than becoming blind.

The surgery had a more profound effect on my personality than we had expected. I became less aggressive, more laid-back. I felt that I had a new lease on life. I enjoyed the sunsets and the simple things, eating an ice cream, lying in bed with my wife and seeing if I could perform. It was like being re-born.

I began questioning my whole life. What was I doing, why was I there? This was an inconvenient time to do that since I had just started a new job as a full Professor, but I was distracted by things that previously I would have glossed over or not even noticed. In re-thinking my life I came to two conclusions, the first and obvious one was never to take things for granted, and the second was that although I was very lucky I was not in the ideal place for me.

I had always harbored an idea of moving to Israel. I had always been a Zionist in principle, but had never managed to get around to it in practice. Now with no kids at home and a good job from which to start I began to consider this possibility.

~~~~~~~~~~~~~

I had lived in Israel before. When I had been a student studying biochemistry in London I had applied for a NATO post-doctoral Fellowship to go abroad. On impulse where it asked for the country you wished to study in I had written "Israel." Later when I went for an interview one of the Professors had asked me why I had selected Israel, and I said that as a Jew I wanted an opportunity to visit and work there, and also I had found a lab in the Weizmann Institute in Rehovot that did high level work in exactly the area I was interested in. Furthermore, I had written to the head of the lab and had received a positive reply from him. The interviewer pointed out that Israel is not a NATO country and no-one had previously gone to work there on a NATO Fellowship. But, nevertheless they seemed to be impressed by my forthright reply.

I was ecstatic when I received the Fellowship, I ran around the room kissing the letter. This was going to be the first big adventure of my life. I decided to spend the whole summer vacation making my way slowly to Israel. I had already found three potential fellow travelers, Martin Lipsett, an economics student, who had some cousins in Israel he had never met, Anne Graham, a Cambridge girl who wanted to see the world, and although not Jewish seemed to like to be with Jews, and Robert Klein a mathematician. Together we bought an old mini-bus and provisioned it out and made the necessary arrangements and started the journey from London.

Everything went smoothly until we camped overnight on the shore of a lake in Switzerland. We had arrived when it was already dark so we could not see where we were. Unluckily for us we camped at a base of a huge sloping foothill of a mountain. During the night at about 2 am we were awakened by a howling storm. We fought to keep the tent down, but to no avail, it was torn away and we were exposed to the drenching rain and raging flood. We struggled to save what we could and then ran for safety to the nearby building, where we sheltered with others throughout the night. In the morning we collected our possessions, rung them out and hung them out to dry as we went streaming down the highway.

But, our luck had begun to run out. Just before Como the engine started to cut out, and then start up again, until finally it stopped completely. We slowed to a halt just above Como. We decided the easiest thing was to push it downhill into Como and find the nearest garage. We did this, but when we found one it turned out that it was siesta time and the mechanics were all going off duty. So we went for a walk down to the lake, had an ice cream and hung around until they returned.

After a few hours and a lot of lira we were on our way. A small problem with the water pump. But hours later on the Autostrada del Sol it started again. Gradually the cutting out of the engine grew worse until we ground to a halt. The police came by and had us towed to the nearest garage. There was one mechanic, and between pumping gas he gradually went through every component of the engine. We were all ready to give up, making other arrangements. But he persevered, and eventually came to the conclusion by process of elimination that it was the simplest possible problem, dirt in the fuel lead. When he bypassed the fuel line with a plastic pipe, the engine raced beautifully. We asked him how much we owed him for his hours of work and he said practically nothing. We paid him more anyway, but we were ecstatic to finally be on the road again racing south.

I don't know why but this minor incident has stayed in my mind. I found myself remembering it with happiness when lying in bed recovering from my operation. What did it represent? There I am sitting in the passenger seat with the sun dappling through the trees, and a sense of infinite possibilities, of release, of freedom attained.

Lesser Known Heroes of Jewish History

"Let us now praise famous men" - Ecclesiastes

Everyone has heard of famous Jewish heroes like Moses, Albert Einstein, Sigmund Freud and David Ben Gurion. But, there is another group of Jewish heroes who are not so well known, who nevertheless deserve to be recognized for their important contributions to Jewish and general history. This article sprang out of my interest in those Jews, and a few non-Jews, who had played an important, even a heroic, role in Jewish history, but are relatively unknown, or even obscure.

I have collected a *partial* list of such people, who were the subjects of several lectures I have given over the years. Among the most deserving I have selected *fourteen*, all of whom merit consideration. A fuller list would include such luminaries as: *Dona Gracia Nasi* (1510-1569), Jewish proto-feminist and wealthy banker; *Nahum Sokolow* (1859-1936), Zionist leader, author and assistant to Chaim Weizmann; *Hillel Kook* (aka Peter Bergson) (1915-2001), Palestinian Jewish representative in the USA before WWII; *Col. Orde Wingate* (1903-1944), military advisor to the early Zionists; *Irena Sendler* (1910-2008), savior of Jewish children during the Holocaust, and so on. These and many more deserve to be included, but space limitations constrain me to choose a selected number of them for inclusion here (below). I find these perhaps the most colorful, interesting and amazing personalities.

Unfortunately, there is not enough space to provide full biographies of these deserving people, but it is hoped that these brief portraits will lead the reader to seek fuller biographies elsewhere (see bibliographies).

Leon Pinsker (1821-1891) Zionist author and pioneer

Pinhas Rutenberg (1879-1942) Socialist revolutionary and founder of the Israel Electric Corporation

Bronislaw Huberman (1882-1947) Violinist and organizer of the Israel Philharmonic Orchestra

Sholom Schwartzbard (1886-1938) Assassin of Simon Petlyura, Ukrainian nationalist

Morris "Two-Gun" Cohen (1887-1970) Bodyguard to Pres. Sun Yat Sen of China

Isaac Rosenberg (1890-1918) British WWI poet

Shmuel Zieglboim (1895-1943) Jewish representative to the Polish Govt. in exile during WWII

Leopold Trepper (1904-1982) Soviet spy chief in Europe during WWII

Sir Solly Zuckerman (1904-1993) British scientific leader

Tuvia Bielski (1906-1987) Partisan leader during WWII

Delmore Schwartz (1913-1966) American poet and writer

Zvika Greengold (1952-   ) Israeli military hero

Non-Jews who played an important role in Jewish History

Richard Meinertzhagen (1878-1967) British spy and representative in Palestine

Josiah DuBois (1913-1983) American lawyer and Holocaust savior

൞ ൞

Leon Pinsker (1821-1891)

Leon Pinsker grew up in Odessa and had a Jewish-secular education. He was a physician, author and Zionist pioneer. He famously published "*Auto-Emancipation*" in 1882 that preceded Herzl's famous "*Altneuland*" by 20 years. Pinsker founded the *Hovevei Zion* (Lovers of Zion) movement and organized its first conference in Katovice in 1884. This resulted in ca. 80,000 Jews making aliyah. He greatly influenced the subsequent Zionist movement.

There were several possible responses to the predicament of the Jews of Europe, and it became urgent for the Jewish elite to resolve this problem, since many of them foresaw disaster ahead. One response was socialism or communism, the belief that all men are brothers, in other words "internationalism," and that national identity did not matter, but in fact it did. Another response was "territorialism" the belief that the Jews should have their own separate nation state in Europe, but this was a non-starter. Another approach was proposed in 1882 by Leo Pinsker a Russian Jew who published a small but influential pamphlet entitled "*Auto-Emancipation*."

What Pinsker said in this pamphlet was that the Jews should not depend on the surrounding peoples to grant them emancipation, but the Jews must emancipate themselves, they must become a nation like other nations, and expect equality with them as individuals and as a group. It is noteworthy that in his proposal, he says nothing about Judaism, he is not interested in religion per se, he is trying to formulate a path whereby Jews and the Jewish people can be physically saved, both from assimilation and from persecution.

These views were echoed in 1896 by Theodor Herzl, an assimilated Jewish journalist who wrote for a Viennese paper and covered the Dreyfus trial in 1895. The widespread anti-Semitism that Herzl experienced in France convinced him that the hatred of the Jews was irrational and was not religious, but was racial. He felt that the Jews could not survive in that atmosphere in Europe for very long, and so he formulated his views in a pamphlet entitled "*The Jewish State: A search for a modern solution to the Jewish question.*" In this work Herzl took Pinsker's proposal to its logical conclusion, in order to achieve full auto-emancipation the Jews needed to have their own nation state, not an artificial one carved out of Europe, but the return to a modern version of the Jewish State in its original location, in Zion. Thus was born political Zionism, and the first Zionist Congress took place in Basle in 1898, when Herzl famously declared "today I have taken the first steps to found the Jewish State," it took a mere 50 years.

It is important to note that the founders of the Zionist movement were not predominantly religious in their motivation, but they were predominantly nationalists, like Zeev Jabotinsky, or, even though the majority of Jewish socialists were internationalists, some were socialist-nationalists, such as Ber Borochov, who quoted the Talmud "If liberation is carried out in Eretz Yisrael then it is carried out everywhere." He was followed by others, including David Ben Gurion, so the nation State of Israel was founded by predominantly secular Jewish intellectuals. Unfortunately, the vast majority of European Jews remained impervious or opposed to this process, remaining either traditional or attempting to fully assimilate. The tragic processes of history revealed in time that political Zionism was in fact the only effective answer to the Jewish predicament and it was initiated by Leon Pinsker.

For a biography of Leon Pinsker see the entry in the *YIVO Encyclopaedia of Jews of Eastern Europe* and references therein.

෴

Pinhas Rutenberg (1879-1942)

Pinhas Rutenberg was born in Ukraine and studied in St. Petersburg, where he became a member of the Socialist-Revolutionary (SR) Party. He became a friend of Father George Gapon who was a leader of the

SR Party and unknown to his colleagues was also an agent of the Czarist secret police (the Okhrana). On Bloody Sunday, 1905, Rutenberg was with Gapon who had organized a worker's march to the Winter Palace. The Army fired on the marchers and this sparked the 1905 revolution. Rutenberg and Gapon managed to escape and fled to France, where they were met by prominent Socialist leaders, including Vladimir Lenin and Georges Clemenceau.

Gapon admitted to Rutenberg that he was a police agent and tried to recruit him. Rutenberg told his SR colleagues about this and they arranged to meet Gapon at an isolated place. Gapon was then found hanged, Rutenberg blamed the SR leaders for his death, but they blamed Rutenberg and he was expelled from the Party. Rutenberg was forced to leave Russia and settled in Italy. He studied hydraulic engineering and during this period became a Zionist. After WWI broke out Rutenberg collaborated with Zionist leader Vladimir Jabotinsky to organize a Jewish armed force to fight for the Holy Land. He toured the US in order to obtain support and funding for this venture. He also published a book entitled *"The National Revival of the Jewish People."* While in the US he developed a detailed design for utilization of the hydraulic resources of the Land of Israel for irrigation and electrical production.

When the second Russian revolution occurred in February 1917, Rutenberg returned to Russia and was appointed VP of the Petrograd municipality (Duma) by the SR PM Alexander Kerensky. The head of the Petrograd Soviet was Leon Trotsky. The Duma and the Soviet were at loggerheads and in October the Bolshevik revolution took place. Kerensky managed to escape but all his followers including Rutenberg were arrested. They were later released, but the Bosheviks instituted the "Red terror" against the SR party members and in 1919 Rutenberg managed to escape to Paris.

There Rutenberg proposed his electrification scheme for Palestine and received funding from the Rothschilds. Rutenberg then settled in Palestine, but his first project together with Jabotinsky was to organize a Jewish self-defense force that later became the Haganah. Rutenberg commanded these forces in Tel Aviv during the Arab uprising of 1921.

Rutenberg obtained a concession from the British Mandate to supply electricity to Jaffa in 1923 and gradually developed a grid to cover all of Palestine. He founded the Palestine Electric Company with the support of the Colonial Secretary Winston Churchill and he invited Lord Reading to be on his board with other noted individuals. He built the Reading power station outside Tel Aviv and the hydroelectric plant at Naharayim on the Jordan River. Rutenberg died in 1942 in Jerusalem and after the founding of the State, the Palestine Electric Company became the Israel Electric Corporation. A large modern power station near Ashkelon is named after him.

For more information about Pinhas Rutenberg see: *"The electrification of Palestine,"* Ronen Shamir, Stanford Univ. Press, 2013.

Bronislaw Huberman (1882-1947)

Bronislaw Huberman was born in Czestochowa, Poland, in 1882 and at an early age was recognized as a violin prodigy. His father took him to Berlin where he studied with the greatest violinists and he was soon touring the world and played in Britain, the USA and Russia. In the 1920s he was recognized as the greatest violinist of his generation.

He was deeply affected by the suffering of WWI and was active in founding the Pan-European society that espoused peace through national reconciliation. In 1926 he visited Palestine, then under British control, and performed throughout the country to enthusiastic Jewish audiences. However, the growth of Nazism in the 1930s took him and many others by surprise. After 1933 he refused to perform in Germany, even though he was personally invited by Adolf Hitler.

During the consolidation of Nazi power in Germany, Jews were dismissed from all professional posts and this included some of the greatest musicians. Wilhelm Furtwangler, the famous conductor of the Berlin Philharmonic Orchestra, although he was sympathetic to the plight of the Jewish musicians, he nevertheless cooperated with the Nazis and all the Jews in the Orchestra were fired. Huberman seeing the plight of so many top Jewish musicians, out of work with no source of income and having been in Palestine and experienced the thirst there for European music, realized that he could do something about the situation. He conceived the idea of establishing a first-class orchestra in Palestine made up of the Jewish musicians who were now available in Europe. He also foresaw the catastrophe that was looming for the Jews of Europe, and so he took upon himself the project of not only founding this orchestra, but of saving the lives of the Jewish musicians, not only of Germany, but of all Europe.

During the early 1930s, as the situation in Germany worsened, Huberman spent several years criss-crossing Europe auditioning Jewish musicians for the planned Palestine Orchestra. He did this to the detriment of his own musical career. For many of the Jewish musicians the idea of going to Palestine, which at that time was considered a God-forsaken country, full of sand and Arabs and not much else, was too much and even though they had no work and were in danger many rejected the offer, they were not Zionists. In response to the situation in Germany a Jewish orchestra was organized to play for exclusively Jewish audiences with the permission of the SS, but that did not last long. Huberman gradually accumulated a list of the premier musicians in Europe and then came the very difficult task of ensuring their entry into Palestine.

In order to enter Palestine a Jew needed two documents, a visa from the British Mandatory Government and permission from the Jewish Agency. Both proved to be very difficult to obtain, since both had restrictions. David Ben Gurion, the Head of the JA in Palestine refused to issue permits to Huberman for the musicians since he gave preference to workers and fighters, since that was what the Zionist cause needed. So Huberman went over his head to the Chairman of the JA, Chaim Weizmann in London, and he was persuaded to issue the permits. Weizmann also contacted the British Government in London who agreed to the entry. The then British High Commissioner of Palestine Arthur Wauchope agreed to issue special exemption certificates for all the musicians and their immediate families, so after several months everything looked clear. But, Huberman lacked the money to pay for the travel and other expenses of the musicians and the setting up of the Orchestra. So he persuaded Albert Einstein to sponsor a dinner in New York that collected enough funds. He also persuaded Arturo Toscanini, the premier conductor in the world, who was an active anti-Nazi, to conduct the Orchestra

So Huberman gathered some 100 musicians in Tel Aviv, 30 from Poland, 25 from Germany, 5 from Holland and Czechoslovakia and so on. They gave their inaugural concert in Tel Aviv on March, 1936 under maestro Toscanini, and it was a huge success. The concert was broadcast all over the world and was heard from Berlin to Los Angeles. The Orchestra toured Palestine giving concerts, and Ben Gurion had to admit that it was a tremendous success for Zionism. What Huberman wanted was to establish the continuity of European Jewish culture that very much included music in the Holy Land. When Israel was established in 1948 the Orchestra changed its name to the Israel Philharmonic Orchestra, recognized as one of the greatest Orchestras in the world. Through his efforts Huberman not only established the IPO, but also saved the lives of an estimated 1,000 Jews, including the musicians and their families. Huberman, exhausted by his efforts, died in 1947 in Switzerland.

For a biography of Bronislaw Huberman see: "*Orchestra of Exiles,*" documentary film produced by Josh Aronson, 2012.

Sholom Schwartzbard (1886-1938)

Simon Petlyura was the leader of the Ukrainian nationalists in the early 20th century and Head of the Ukrainian National Republic in 1919. During his reign in the Ukraine, before the Bolsheviks took over, his troops massacred ca. 50,000 Jews. There are conflicting reports of whether or not Petlyura ordered this or he just let his troops get on with it. On his orders one of the leaders of the pogroms was arrested and later executed, but this did not stop the massacres.

Later he was ousted by the Soviets and fled to Paris in 1924. In Paris in 1925 he was assassinated by Sholom Schwartzbard, an anarchist, whose family had been massacred in Odessa by the Ukrainians under Petlyura.

Schwartzbard was born in Odessa and led a very colorful life, in his teens he became a socialist and fought in Jewish self-defense units. He was arrested and imprisoned, but then released and was forced to flee Ukraine He worked in Austria and elsewhere and ended up in France in 1910, where he married and joined the French Foreign Legion and fought in WWI and earned the Croix de Guerre in 1917. He was a writer of Yiddish poetry under the pen name of "The Dreamer" and one of his books was called "*Dreams and Reality.*"

In 1917 he travelled to Russia and became part of an anarchist group that fought with the Red Guards against the Czar's forces in St. Petersburg, but was later denounced by the Bolsheviks and forced to flee back to Ukraine. There in 1919 he saw first-hand the pogroms of the Petlyura regime. He managed to escape and get a boat and returned to France.

When he heard that Petlyura had also arrived in Paris he plotted his assassination. It is suspected that he was assisted by Bolshevik agents in this quest. In 1925 he shot Petlura eight times on a street in Paris. In the ensuing trial in 1927 his defence was that Petlyura had been responsible for the massacre of his family and many thousands of Jews, and he was acquitted in 1928.

He was famous among Jews and known as "the avenger" (*hanokem*). He emigrated to Palestine in 1928 and travelled to the US and South Africa to raise funds for various projects, including a Yiddish encyclopedia. He died in Cape Town in 1938. In accordance with his will, his remains were transported to Israel in 1967, where he is buried in Moshav Avihayil outside Netanya. There are streets named after him (*Rehov Hanokem*) in several Israeli cities, including Jerusalem and Beersheva.

For further biographical details see the *YIVO Encyclopedia of Jews of Eastern Europe*.

అ ఈ

Morris "Two Gun" Cohen (1887-1970)

Morris ("Mickey") Abraham Cohen was born in 1887 in the East End of London. From his earliest years he was a difficult child and grew us as a tough street kid. He was sent to a remand home for wayward boys and was rescued by the Jewish Welfare Board and with his parents agreement was sent to Canada to live with his Uncle who had a farm there. But, his uncle preferred to hire him out to the large Nicholson ranch. There he learnt to ride and shoot and became used to carrying a gun. After a few years he left and went to the nearest city

Edmonton, where he survived on his wits as a small time crook.

He became involved in gambling and came into contact with the Chinese community. The Chinese were greatly discriminated against and particularly the Police Chief was very biased against them. Morris developed good relations with the Chinese and fronted for them in gambling and real estate deals, where he took a percentage, but was scrupulously honest. He also took steps to undermine the Police Chief, for which the Chinese were very grateful. Perhaps as a result of his being a Jew he sympathized with the Chinese predicament and became involved in their businesses as a white front-man. He had a reputation of being tough but honest. He hired himself out as a body-guard and it was at this time that he took to carrying two guns, one obvious on his belt and another hidden, hence the nickname "Two-Gun" Cohen. The Chinese inducted him into their Tong or secret society and he learnt some Mandarin.

During WWI Cohen joined the Canadian Army and was transferred to France. There the British forces had problems building railways to transfer supplies for the troops and they used Chinese labor, but could not get them to work efficiently. Someone had heard of this Canadian who could speak Mandarin, so Cohen was seconded to the Transportation unit, in charge of the Chinese and in short time he improved their conditions and had them working effectively. After the War he visited London and then returned to Edmonton.

At this time, Sun Yat Sen, the founder of the Chinese Republican movement, took up residence in Vancouver after being expelled from China. A delegation of Chinese went from Edmonton to meet Sen and Cohen went with them. Sen was fascinated by this young white man who could speak some Mandarin and was vouched for by the Edmonton Chinese. He was tough and reliable, so Sen hired Cohen as his bodyguard to accompany him on his trip to Washington and then throughout the US and Canada. It was natural then that when the circumstances changed and Sen was able to return to Canton as the President of the Chinese Republic that he would take "Two-Gun" Cohen with him.

Cohen not only remained a bodyguard of Pres. Sen, but also fronted for him in various deals, including the building of railways and the importation of arms ("gun-runing"). It was at this time, as an influential person in the Chinese hierarchy, that Cohen became a spy for the British centered in Hong Kong. During the wars that accompanied the establishment of the Chinese Republic, Cohen played a role and for this was promoted to the honorary rank of General in the Chinese Republican Army and was called Mah Kun by the Chinese.

Cohen was also sent by Pres. Sen on various missions where he could pass because he was *not* Chinese. In an anecdote that could not be corroborated, he was sent to Beijing to secretly negotiate on behalf of Pres. Sen with the war-lord who controlled northern China. He posed as an arms dealer and managed to get access to the General, but then they realized that they did not have a common language. The General did not speak English and spoke a different dialect of Chinese. But, it turned out that the General had studied in Germany and had lived for several years in the house of a Jewish family. The negotiation on behalf of the Chinese Government was carried out in Yiddish.

The Chinese Republic grew, but then Pres. Sen died in 1925 and Cohen's role diminished as he was not trusted by Sen's successor, Gen. Chiang Kai Shek. Then the threat of the Japanese grew. They first occupied Manchuria in 1931 and established the puppet state of Manchuoko. Then at the start of WWII they attacked and occupied Shanghai, Hong Kong and much of China. After choosing not to flee, Cohen was captured and was interned and interrogated. However, he gave nothing away and persuaded them that he knew nothing, and so spent several years in a prison camp. He was exchanged for Japanese prisoners held by the Allies and was repatriated to Canada in 1944, where he was hailed as a hero.

He lived in Toronto, but as the Communists won the war against the Nationalists in 1949, Cohen's star in China waned. However, Madame Sen, the wife of the former

President, became the Minister of Education in the Communist Government of Mao Tse Tung, and she vouched for Cohen, although he had been an ardent anti-Communist. Nevertheless he was able to visit China in 1955, and he published glowing accounts of his visit. But, he never regained anything like his former glory and retired to Toronto, where he died in obscurity in 1970.

For biographies of Morris Cohen see: *"Two-Gun Cohen,"* Charles Drage, Jonathan Cape, London, 1954; *"Two-Gun Cohen"* by Daniel S. Levy, St. Martin's Press, NY 1997.

Isaac Rosenberg (1890-1918)

Isaac Rosenberg was a British Jewish poet of WWI. He was born poor in Bristol and went to London to study art. A chance meeting at the National Gallery resulted in an older lady paying for his art courses at the Slade School. His life was short and seemingly simple. He made a trip to S. Africa and while he was there WWI was declared. He returned to London, enlisted in the British Army in 1914 and was killed fighting in the trenches in 1918 at the age of 28.

Throughout his short life he wrote poetry, and it is for this that he has belatedly become famous, after a gap of over 60 years. He wrote a series of "poems from the trenches," that in their "fierce immediacy" have resulted in experts on WWI poets such as Jon Silkin (see "*Poetry of the First World War*") to declare him perhaps the greatest of them all. Here is one example, a wonderful metaphor for a bullet from "*Dead Man's Dump*"

> "*Out of those doomed nostrils and the doomed mouth,*
> *Where the swift iron burning bee*
> *Drained the wild honey of their youth.*"

Other examples: "*Marching*"
> *My eyes catch ruddy necks*
> *Sturdily pressed back –*
> *All a red brick moving glint*
> *Live flaming pendulums, hands*
> *Swinging across the khaki –*
> *Mustard-coloured khaki –*
> *To the automatic feet*

Also, "*Break of day in the trenches*"
> *The darkness crumbles away*
> *It is the same old Druid time as ever.*
> *Only a live thing leaps my hand –*
> *A queer sardonic rat –*
> *As I pull the parapet's poppy*
> *To stick behind my ear.*
> *Droll rat, they would shoot you if they knew*
> *Your cosmopolitan sympathies.*

Why was Rosenberg ignored for so long? Because he was Jewish in WWI England, because he was poor, because he was a private when the other famous poets, Wilfrid

Owen, Siegfied Sasoon, etc., were officers, and because he died young. Although he died in obscurity, he is now acknowledged as a great poet and there is a plaque recognizing him on the wall outside the Whitechapel Library in East London where he worked.

For biographies of Isaac Rosenberg see: "*Isaac Rosenberg, poet and painter*," Jean Moorcroft Wilson, Cecil Woolf, London, 1975; "*Isaac Rosenberg*," Vivian Noakes, Oxford, 2012

ઊ ૭

Shmuel Ziegelboim (1895-1943)

Shmuel Ziegelboim was one of two Jewish representatives to the Polish Government in exile in London during WWII. He tried desperately, but in vain, to try to awaken public opinion to the atrocities being conducted against Polish Jewry by the Nazis.

When the news arrived of the extermination of the Warsaw Ghetto, Ziegelboim committed suicide outside the Houses of Parliament in London on May 12, 1943, in protest at the passivity with which the world was permitting the Nazis to destroy the Jews of Europe.

Before his death he wrote a letter to the President of Poland, he wrote "I cannot live while the remnants of the Jewish people in Poland, whose representative I am, are being exterminated." For his heroic, doomed act, Shmuel Ziegelboim should be honored and remembered.

For an article about Shmuel Ziegelboim, see the entry in the *YIVO Encyclopedia of Jews of Eastern Europe* and references therein.

Leopold Trepper (1904-1982)

Leopold Trepper was born in Poland in 1904 and was educated at the University of Krakow. Unable to find any work, he ended up as a miner and soon became an organizer of the miners and a dedicated communist. He was arrested by the authorities and spent 9 months in prison. After his release in 1928, because it was dangerous for him to stay there, he joined a Zionist organization and emigrated to Palestine. There he continued his communist activities, organizing anti-British strikes, and was once again arrested and expelled back to Europe. In France he joined a Communist spy-ring gathering information for the KGB in Moscow. He changed his identity several times and had passports under pseudonyms such as Leiba Domb.

His abilities were noted and in 1932 he was called to Moscow for training. He returned to Belgium in 1938 tasked with setting up a spy ring mainly targeted on the British. Trepper established companies using legitimate businessmen as fronts, such as the "Excellent Trenchcoat Company" with a branch in Ostend. But, with foresight, Trepper realized that the Germans would be the main enemy of the Soviet Union and so he extended his activities to Paris. Sooner than he expected the Germans conquered France and occupied Paris, and in 1940 Trepper, under the name of Jean Gilbert, was put in charge of all Soviet intelligence in occupied Europe. Trepper spoke fluent German, French and Russian as well as Polish and Hebrew. He had a group in Berlin led by two dedicated communists, Harro Schultze-Boysen and Arvid Harnack, as well as networks in Brussels and Paris, amounting to 279 members, of whom 66 were Jews.

Trepper cultivated contacts particularly with SS officers, who received lavish presents and attended parties run by Trepper's companies, such as Simexco in Paris. Information collected thru these contacts was transferred to Moscow by radio transmitters. They gave invaluable information to Moscow, including the date of the German invasion of Russia, June 22, 1941, and the specifications of the German Tiger tank. Since the radio operators were called "pianists" the whole spy ring was called an Orchestra and its conductor was Trepper.

The Germans were furious when they realized that a transmitter was operating out of Berlin, and they also discovered with horror that there were transmitters with similar call signs operating out of Brussels and

Paris. It took them some time to get organized due to inter-agency competition as well as technical difficulties. But, eventually the Gestapo discovered the spy rings in Berlin and in Brussels and Paris. Many members of the spy ring were captured, tortured and eventually executed. One of Trepper's main agents in Brussels Hersh Sokol was hung upside down in a cell and dogs were set upon him, however, he did not talk. Eventually the Gestapo caught up with Trepper and he was arrested in Paris in 1942.

The Gestapo did not realize that Gilbert, alias Trepper, was Jewish. They treated him with consideration as the head of the Soviet spy ring in Europe and turned him, persuaded him to send disinformation to Moscow in order to deceive them. He called this "the great game" and used it as the title of his autobiography. During WWII Trepper had led a high life, using the black market to make money and bribe people, and he did not share the terrible fate of his collaborators. This led some to question his loyalty, although he claimed after the war that he had always been a loyal anti-Nazi.

Over time he gained the confidence of his handlers, and even though he was always accompanied by two SS guards, he managed to escape from them in 1944. He got them used to going to a pharmacy to get drugs he needed, and then one day he vanished because he knew that there was another entrance to that pharmacy. He used safe houses to make his way across Europe and managed to pass thru Germany and across the front lines into Soviet-occupied territory.

But, when he arrived in Moscow he was arrested and imprisoned by Stalin, who trusted no-one, especially those who had been in contact with the Germans. He spent 8 years in Soviet prisons, until the death of Stalin in 1953. Then he was released, and chose to return to Poland and was appointed Chairman of the Jewish Community organization in Warsaw in 1955. He remained there until he could leave in 1973 and died in Jerusalem in 1982.

The *Jerusalem Post* dated Dec 24, 1988 (p. 9), published an article by Jon Immanuel entitled "*The Palestinian Jew who spied for Stalin*." There is a grove of trees in the Sha'ar Hagai forest near Jerusalem commemorating Trepper and the other members of the Red Orchestra. None other than Himmler himself estimated that the work of the Red Orchestra had cost Germany the lives of 200,000 soldiers during WWII. Let this be his memorial. Leopold Trepper exemplified the resourceful, tough Jew who showed that Jews if organized could exact a great price from our enemies.

For a book about Leopold Trepper see: "*The Red Orchestra*" by Gilles Perrault, Simon & Shuster, 1967

Solly Zuckerman (1904-1993)

Solly Zuckerman grew up in South Africa in a middle class Jewish family. Once he had qualified as a biology major by studying a colony of baboons in the Veldt, he moved by himself to Britain in 1926. Britain was the mecca for all aspiring subjects from the colonies. Solly could not have known that he would become one of the most powerful men in England, and during WWII would be responsible for important areas of Defense policy.

From the start Solly was a bit of a social climber, he quickly attached himself to wealthy and important people, including the Jewish Lord and Lady Melchett, Isaiah Berlin, J.D. Bernal, etc. People found him charming, knowledgeable, and driven. He worked incredible hours, and soon was successful in his PhD program in London on the skull of baboons, not a topic one would think would make him powerful and famous. But, people noted his drive and capability. He was a consummate scientist, basing his conclusions purely on the evidence. When the Ministry of Defense wanted a mammalian biologist to study the effects of blast on humans, Solly submitted a proposal and got the job, using baboons as a model. He showed that most current ideas about the effects of blast were wrong.

He set up a unit in Oxford to gather all known evidence on the subject. He went back to S. Africa for further studies, and was reunited with his family, but apart from a few short visits in the ensuing years he cut himself off from them, as if that connection was an embarrassment to him. Although he never denied his Jewishness, it seemed not to matter much to him.

In experiments that could not be done today, he systematically studied the effects of bomb blasts on baboons, experiments that the Nazis and the Japanese in Manchuria did on humans. In this way he became one of the few men in the world who knew about this subject in a scientific way, and became an invaluable asset when WWII started. In a period of 5 years he published with his staff 90 scientific papers. When the war started he and Bernal initiated a study of the casualties of the German bombing and issued a monograph that became the authority on the subject.

In 1943 he was seconded to the command of Air Field Marshal Lord Tedder in North Africa, and from the start they got along very well. It proved most important for Solly's future to have such a powerful patron. Solly was asked to assess the effectiveness of bombs on gun emplacements, how badly damaged were the guns, the surroundings and the number of men killed. He quickly realized that the American bombs were more effective at causing damage and killing the gunners, and he proved that this was because the American bomb fuses were set to go off a few seconds after impact, while the British ones were set for the instant of impact. He argued that the British should change their fuses, something the hardened military men would not do, until Tedder was convinced by the evidence and ordered this done throughout the theatre of war. Next, Tedder gave him the job of coming up with a plan to capture the heavily fortified island of Pantelleria, off the coast of N. Africa, which was needed before the Allies could commence the invasion of Sicily. Solly studied photos of the island, and proposed a massive bombing campaign to save the lives of men in a suicide attack on the heavily defended island. Tedder, against advice by his military chiefs, adopted this plan, and ordered the RAF to concentrate its bombers on Pantelleria. Solly had calculated that if more than 25% of the island's defenses could be destroyed the Germans would give in, and in fact they did, almost without a fight. This was considered a great coup for Solly and made him famous as a technical advisor.

When Tedder moved back to England to run the air campaign of the invasion of Europe under Eisenhower, he took Solly with him. After careful study of all air aspects of the invasion Solly advised a coordinated powerful bombing attack on all communications and railways, to prevent rapid German reaction to the invasion force. But, Bomber Command, under Gen 'Bomber' Harris had adopted a strategy of hitting German cities, believing that they could thus break German morale and win the war quickly.

Solly studied the evidence and found that German production had in fact increased during the period of the intensive city bombing campaign. He also took evidence from the German bombing of British cities and showed that it was not valid. However, powerful forces were at play, and the top military brass did not appreciate an upstart technician (and a Jew at that) telling them what to do. Nevertheless, once again Tedder and eventually Eisenhower and Churchill were persuaded by Solly's evidence and a campaign of hitting the northern French railway system was adopted as the precursor to the Normandy Landings. It was a great success, German reinforcements were unable to reach the D-Day landings and many Allied lives were saved.

After WWII Solly was appointed Chairman of the Anatomy Department at Birmingham University, and concurrently he was appointed Chief Scientific Adviser to the Min. of Defense, two full time jobs. He managed this by working in London Mon-Thurs and in Birmingham Fri-Sun. With able staff in both places, carefully selected by him, he managed to carry out both jobs successfully. He married at this time Joan Rufus Isaacs, daughter of Lord Reading and granddaughter of the former Viceroy of India. But, his first love was clearly his work, and his wife recognized that she had married a workaholic.

After a few years he was appointed Chief Scientific Adviser to the British Government, a post he held for 20 years. He was also chosen as the head of the London

Zoo, which became his lifelong devotion. Once again he managed to juggle these two full time jobs, as well as many academic and Government functions. One of his important contributions was being instrumental in 1961 in persuading NATO and the US that the use of "tactical" atomic weapons was unacceptable. He was also responsible for the establishment of the first Department of Environmental Studies in the UK. Solly was a well-known bon vivant, raconteur and name-dropper. He was first knighted as Sir Solly Zuckerman, and then raised to the peerage as Lord Zuckerman. He knew everyone who was important and everyone knew him. His place in history has now been eclipsed, but for a few years his star shone brightly in the firmament of British society.

For a biography of Solly Zuckerman see: "*Solly Zuckerman: a scientist out of the ordinary*," by John Peyton, John Murray, 2001.

Tuvia Bielski (1906-1987)

In Eastern Europe during WWII partisan bands fought the Germans behind enemy lines. Among these were several all-Jewish partisan groups, the largest of which was reputedly that of the Bielski brothers, that was active in the forests of Byelorussia during 1941-44.

The three Bielski brothers started to organize armed resistance against the German invaders when their parents and two younger brothers were murdered and they realized that the Nazis planned to kill all the Jews. They had grown up in the area around the village of Stankevich near the town of Novogrudek in northwestern Byelorussia. Their father owned the largest mill in the area, and the brothers knew and were well-known to all the local population. Two things distinguished the brothers, they would take no anti-Semitic slurs from anyone and they were known to have a violent streak. Of the brothers, Tuvia the oldest, was the most impressive, he was tall and handsome and moved with ease in the world. Asael and Zus were more earthy and confrontational and stayed at home running the mill. When the Germans invaded Byelorussia (now Belarus) Tuvia was working in the nearby town of Lida. He placed his wife and child in the home of a non-Jew he trusted, and went to see what was happening at the mill, only to find that his parents had been taken and his brothers later arrested in town. This was the first stage of the German onslaught against the Jews.

The next stage was the Einsatzcommando, or mobile Special Commandos, whose job it was to go from place to place and kill as many Jews as possible (since this was not efficient enough, the third stage was the extermination camps). The new German civil authority established Ghettos in Novogrudek and Lida and forced as many Jews into them as possible. Then with local troops and the Einsatzcommandos, they removed all the Jews who could not work and took them to pre-prepared graves in the forest and shot them all dead, including children. In this way some 3,500 Jews were murdered in Lida and 5,000 in Novogrudek. Tuvia Bielski's wife and child were among those murdered. The Bielski brothers knew about these events from their contacts in the Byelorussian community and from a few Jewish escapees, some of whom went to their mill to seek protection.

In order to survive, the three brothers decided to move into the nearby forest and establish a base there. They recruited several young Jewish men and at first started with about 18 fighters and some 20 non-combatants. Since they knew the area and the forests very well they moved around fairly freely and used a mixture of persuasion and threats to get food and support from the peasants. Some of the peasants were supportive, such as Konstantin Koslovsky who lived close to the forest and assisted Jews who came to him to make contact with the Bielskis. His younger brother worked with the Byelorussian police and passed on information to the Bielskis through his brother, until he was caught and tortured to death. Koslovsky was later awarded a "righteous gentile" award by Yad Vashem.

Other peasants collaborated with the German occupiers, in one incident 10 Bielski fighters slept in the barn of a supposedly friendly peasant. His son was sent to warn the police and a detachment of Germans returned with a force of police and surrounded the barn and killed all of them. In order to maintain his credibility, Tuvia Bielski returned with 70 armed mounted fighters, killed the whole family and burned all their property down. In this way he let it be known that the Jewish fighters would not tolerate betrayal.

The question is, how did they get enough food and guns and ammunition for their fight? The answer is that one of the prime responsibilities of the fighters was to go out foraging to collect by persuasion and force the necessary amount of food they needed for their band. In order to get guns they first relied on buying from locals and stealing from the Germans, but this was clearly insufficient, so they were eventually forced to make contact with the local Soviet partisan groups. They agreed to give them guns in exchange for food and other goods, but eventually this required the Bielskis to formally join the Soviet partisan military structure and show their commitment to Stalin and his policies. They also had to engage in a specific amount of sabotage and armed action against the German occupiers and their collaborators. During the course of the war they killed some 40 Germans and numerous other collaborators.

Bielski, as commander, adopted one unusual policy, that he would take in any Jews, old or lame, in order to ensure Jewish survival. This was contrary to Soviet policy that allowed only fighters, but he managed to persuade his superiors that he was saving "Soviet citizens." Also, while the Bielskis were formally part of the partisan structure, there were many Russian groups that were overtly hostile to a Jewish partisan force, and there were often clashes between them.

Bielski had five enemies to contend with, 1. The Germans, 2. Collaborators among the Byelorussian peasants, 3. The Polish free army that killed Jews as happily as Germans, 4. Anti-Semitic Russian partisans, and 5. Jews within his own band that were either committed communists or criminals out to steal. He managed by a mixture of ruthlessness and charm to gradually build up his band first to ca. 800 Jews and then eventually to ca. 1,200, the largest such group known. At first they established several dugout settlements in the nearby forests. But, when these became known they gradually moved deeper into the forest. When the Germans mounted a large-scale assault against the partisans in the forests of Byelorussia in 1943, they were forced to move thru the swamps into the deepest forests. Once this assault was over they were able to establish a Jewish shtetl called "Jerusalem" in the middle of the deep forest in the middle of Nazi-occupied Europe. Only with the defeat of the German forces on the Eastern front in late 1944, and the arrival of the Red Army did the need for the Bielski Jewish partisan band cease, and the village was disbanded.

Later, fearing arrest by the Soviets for his many failures

to follow strict military protocols, such as allowing religious Jews to establish a synagogue in the camp and punishing Russian partisans who were anti-Semitic, Tuvia and his brothers fled separately to Western Germany with their new wives and thence to Israel. But, things did not work out there for the two older brothers, they were not taken seriously by the Israeli military, and they moved on to the USA, where they ended up as taxi drivers and truckers in NY. Quite a come-down for two men who had once held the fate of thousands in their hands. But, finally they were awarded medals posthumously by the Israeli Govt.

For books about Tuvia Bielski see: *"Defiance: The Bielski Partisans,"* by Nechama Tec, Oxford Univ. Press, 1993, which was made into the movie *"Defiance"*; *"The Bielski Brothers,"* by Peter Duffy, Harper-Collins, 2003.

Richard Meinertzhagen (1878-1967)

Richard Meinertzhagen, a non-Jew, was born in England to a German father and British mother. He chose a military career and was trained as an intelligence officer (spy). He was first sent to East Africa to help put down an uprising. He invited the chief of the restive tribes to a meeting, and when he was not satisfied with his response, he shot him dead. This resulted in more rioting, and so he was recalled to Britain. During WWI he was a Colonel in the British Army on the staff of Gen. Allenby in Egypt. In his memoirs he described a "ruse" that he was involved in, of dropping a satchel near the Turkish lines to convince them that the British would attack again at Gaza, where the Turks were well dug in. But in fact the British sent the Australian Light Horse on a risky attack across the desert to Beersheva. When this was successful, the Turks were outflanked at Gaza and were forced to withdraw.

Because the Versailles Conference after WWI was for countries, the Arabs and Jews could not be represented directly, but were represented by British officers, Col. T.E. Lawrence ("Lawrence of Arabia") represented the Arabs, and Col. Richard Meinertzhagen represented the Jews. As the representative of the Zionist interests at the Conference, Meinertzhagen played a very crucial role in helping to defend the rights of the Zionists. For this he was greatly thanked and appreciated by Chaim Weizmann, who was Chief of the Zionist delegation. After WWI, Meinertzhagen was the representative of the British Foreign Office in Palestine and it is from his letters and reports that we know a great deal of what happened during the Mandate period.

Meinertzhagen was an avid bird watcher and collector and had one of the greatest collections of bird artifacts in the world. But, he was found to have stolen items from the collections of others to enhance his own collection, and as well as having a violent streak, he was proved to also be a self-serving liar. Nevertheless, he played a crucial role in the history of the Zionist enterprise.

For a biography of Richard Meinertzhagen see: "*Richard Meinertzhagen, soldier, scientist and spy*," Mark Cocker, Mandarin, London, 1990.

ಞ ಀ

Delmore Schwartz (1913-1966)

Delmore Schwartz was born and grew up in Brooklyn, NY. He had a relatively unhappy childhood because his parents did not get along. His father was a handsome philanderer and his mother was highly strung and emotional. They were both immigrants from Romania and Delmore grew up in an intensely Jewish environment. His parents divorced when he was nine and this had a profound effect upon him. Throughout his life he struggled with the complex identity of being American and Jewish.

He excelled at school and college and became a poet at an early age. He received early recognition and joined a group of leftist anti-establishment intellectuals who went on to become leaders of their generation. He helped found and later was editor of *Partisan Review* (1943-55) that became the "bible" of the liberal/leftist intelligentsia of New York and throughout the USA. He taught creative writing in many Universities and Colleges in the

Eastern US and wrote for many well-known publications, such as *The New Republic*.

He wrote poetry and short stories and one of his stories, "*In dreams begin responsibilities*," is a classic of its kind and was published in the first issue of *Partisan Review* in 1937. In this story, Delmore, as a teenager, goes into a movie theater and there sees a movie of the first meeting of his father and mother on Coney Island. In the story he tries to prevent them from meeting and then to prevent them from becoming lovers. This was also the title of his first book published in 1938 to general critical acclaim. He was considered to be one of the most gifted young writer's of his generation and portrayed the Jewish middle-class of NYC.

He was known as an excellent conversationalist and bon vivant in the intellectual circles of NYC. Delmore had a reputation for being prickly and sensitive, while also being vain and arrogant. He had many friends, but quarreled with most of them at one time or another. Perhaps because of the failed marriage of his parents he too was a poor husband and his marriage ended in divorce after six years. He continued writing, publishing and reviewing and was recognized as one of the major influences on American literature of the 1930s-40s. He married for a second time in 1948 and this marriage also ended in divorce. He received the Bollinger Prize for his collection of poetry in 1959, the youngest ever recipient. He had an intense friendship with the American poet

Robert Lowell, and they shared an apartment in 1946, but that relationship also ended in recriminations.

Saul Bellow, who was one of his protégé's, wrote a book based on Delmore Schwartz, entitled *"Humboldt's gift"* that won the Pulitzer Prize. A former student, jazz musician Lou Reed, also composed several pieces in his honor. But, unfortunately, in his later years he antagonized most of his friends and died alone in poverty and obscurity in a hotel room in NYC at the age of 52. His was a star that ascended and burnt brightly, but crashed and left little residue.

For a biography of Delmore Schwartz see: *"Delmore Schwartz, the life of an American Poet,"* James Atlas, Avon Books, 1977.

Josiah DuBois (1913-1983)

Beyond the famous individuals who saved thousands of Jewish lives in the Holocaust (*Shoah*), such as Raoul Wallenberg and Oscar Schindler, there are the less famous heroes, some of whom were overlooked and forgotten. Among these were the British Major Frank Foley, the Portuguese Consul in Hungary Sousa Mendes, the Japanese Vice-Consul in Lithuania, Chiune Sugihara, and a Chinese diplomat in Berlin, Feng-Shan Ho, each of whom saved many Jewish lives by providing visas, against the wishes of their Governments. Another, who worked for the US Government in Washington DC and who deserves to be included among them, was Josiah E. DuBois Jr. By his actions he may have saved more Jewish lives than any other righteous gentile.

DuBois was born in Camden, NJ, in 1913 and went on to study law at Penn U. In 1941, at the start of the Holocaust, DuBois was working in the Foreign Funds Control Board of the US Treasury. A request for $170,000 to pay a bribe to rescue 70,000 Jews came to his desk and he immediately approved it and passed it on to the State Dept. He was later horrified to find that State had deliberately delayed dealing with the request, and despite his efforts he was not able to get them to act for five and a half months, by which time the Jews had already been murdered!

This was a shock to him and he started collecting information on the apparently deliberate and systematic actions (and inaction) of the State Department under Asst. Secty. Breckenridge Long, whose policy was later expounded in an intra-department memo of June 1940: "*We can delay and effectively stop for a temporary period of indefinite length the number of immigrants (*i.e. Jews*) into the United States. We could do this by simply advising our consuls to put every obstacle in the way and to require additional evidence and to resort to various administrative devices which would postpone and postpone and postpone the granting of the visas.*" Thus, 90% of the US quota places available to immigrants from countries under German control were never filled. Later Long was caught lying to Congress about the number of visas authorized and was forced to resign in 1944. But, he and other anti-Semites had done irreparable damage to the Jewish people.

In response to this systematic policy, that was never opposed by Secty. of State Cordell Hull or Pres. Roosevelt, Du Bois began to collect information and on 25 December 1943 he wrote a Report to his boss, Treasury Secty. Henry Morgenthau, who happened to be Jewish, but who had deliberately avoided taking up the case of the European Jews with Roosevelt. This now famous case of whistle-blowing was entitled "*Report to the Secretary of the Acquiescence of This Government in the Murder of the Jews.*" To avoid the same kind of bureaucratic silencing that had been going on for those crucial years DuBois told Morgenthau that if the Secretary did not pass his report on to the President he would resign and present the report to a press conference. To avoid problems in the election then due in only 10 months, Roosevelt relented and established the War Refugee Board, of which DuBois was General Counsel, with his colleague John W. Pehle as its Director.

Very quickly the WRB began to take actions to rescue the lives of Jews in Europe by various means, including bribery. This usually required sending money, but they also arranged for Raoul Wallenberg as an emissary under Swedish auspices to help rescue the Jews of Budapest.

They also established havens for Jewish refugees in N. Africa, Sweden and elsewhere, but only one in the USA, at Fort Ontario, New York, that housed a mere 982 Jews.

After the war ended in 1945 it was estimated that the WRB's direct actions had saved ca. 200,000 Jews, and many more had been rescued, ca. 48,000 in Transnistria alone, as well as the 120,000 saved in Budapest. All of this could not have happened if DuBois had not acted on his principles. He ended his crucial Report with these words: "*If men of the temperament and philosophy of Long continue in control of immigration administration, we may as well take down that plaque from the Statue of Liberty and block out the 'lamp beside the golden door.'*" However, WRB director Pehle described the work as "too little, too late".

Later DuBois was part of the legal team of the Nuremberg Trials that prosecuted those who ran I.G. Farben, the chemical company that used slave-labor under the Nazis. He wrote a memoir about this trial entitled *"The Devil's Chemists."* After that he played no further role in these events and his crucial role was almost entirely forgotten until Arthur Morse in his 1968 book mentioned him.

For a biography of Josiah DuBois see: "*Blowing the Whistle on Genocide: Josiah E. DuBois and the struggle for an American response to the Holocaust*," Rafael Medoff, Purdue Univ. Press, 2008.

Zvika Greengold (1952-)

Greengold was born in Kibbutz Lohamei Hagetaot (Fighters of the Ghetto) and was training to be an IDF tank commander at age 21 when the Yom Kippur war broke out in 1973. Since he had not yet been assigned to a unit he hitch-hiked to the Golan Heights front and there he commandeered a repaired tank and with two other loners, he set out towards the front. Because he had no correct designation the communications network called him "Force Zvika." His tank was hit and he was injured, but he changed tanks and continued, something he did four times during the following day.

He was a lone tank and when he crested a hill he saw a huge column of tanks coming towards him, estimated at 150 Syrian tanks. They all had their lights on, presumably because they had reconnoitered the area and found no opposition. Zvika began shooting down on them and then moved his position and shot again and continued doing this for hours, until the valley was blocked by burning tanks, and the rest of the tanks either retreated or were left by their crew.

Zvika single-handedly destroyed 40 Syrian tanks and saved the Golan Heights from being overrun and saved

Israel from a Syrian invasion. There were other heroes of this campaign, such as Avigdor Kahalani, but Zvika fought alone for 20 hours and when reinforcements eventually arrived he collapsed and was taken to hospital. For his heroism he was given Israel's highest military award. Zvika was a child of Holocaust survivors and said that he felt they had survived so that he could be there to fight for and save Israel.

These then are some selected individuals who are generally unknown, but who deserve greater appreciation and recognition for their contributions to Jewish history.

Printed in Great Britain
by Amazon